THE SEXY F

©Copyright – MK Jubb

ALL RIGHTS RESERVED

NO PART OF THIS BOOK MAY BE COPIED IN ANY FORM WITHOUT

PERMISSION FROM COPYRIGHT OWNER, PUBLISHER OR AUTHOR OF THIS BOOK

NAMES AND PLACES ARE FICTIONAL AND ANY SIMULARITIES ARE COINCIDENCE

THE SEXY FAKER

THE SEXY FAKER
BY
MK JUBB

THE SEXY FAKER

Dedicated to my husband for his love & support always

THE SEXY FAKER

THE SEXY FAKER

ANNABELLE

My head hurts so bad. I am never drinking again. I drag the pillow from under my head and put it over my face, groaning when a pain shoots down my temple.
Why do I let Ricky talk me in to shots. I hate them, and they hate me. I'm pretty sure that the bottle he found at the back of the cupboard, was questionable before we even drank it. The smell alone should have put us off, but no, Ricky was like "It's ok, alcohol always smells bad when you're already drunk". Nope, definitely not ok!
So, needless to say, I spent most of the night puking my guts up, before crashing on to Ricky's bed. At some point in the night he had also crashed out on the bed next to me.
I had also come to the conclusion that once I had gotten over my hangover, I was going to kill him. Because now, I am going to have to call in sick to work. The lawyer firm I work for have a big case at the moment, and it is all hands-on deck. They will kill me for pulling a sicky, but not before I have pulverised Ricky first!
What is that banging? It must be my head.
I try to open my eyes, but the idiot forgot to close the curtains, so now there is bright light piercing through my eye

lids. Great! And the banging isn't in my head either. Some idiot has decided to try and knock the door down.

I lift my knee up and flatten my foot on Ricky's back and push hard.

'Arrgh! What are you doing? Stop it'.

'I'll stop when you go stop that idiot who's banging on your door'. I roll over and cover my head again with the pillow.

'Why don't you go answer it?'

'Because it is your apartment dip shit'.

I feel the bed move, but when I crack an eye open, he hasn't gotten out of bed, he's just turned over, facing away from me the bastard.

'SOMEONE, PLEASE MAKE THAT BANGING STOP!' I shout through to one of the other dead to the world body's in the other room.

Yay, the banging has stop.

I wince, when another loud bang blasts in to the room. It appears someone has decided to swing the bedroom door open and letting it bang on the wall. Then said person decides it is a good idea to start shouting at us.

Whoever this asshole is, will be getting it with both barrels!

'WHAT THE FUCK IS GOING ON HERE? ANSWER ME DAMN IT! RICHARD?'

Ok, obviously some friend of Ricky's I don't know. Who the hell does he think he is coming in here like he owns the place and shouting like that?

THE SEXY FAKER

'HEY, BUDDY. KEEP THE FUCKING SHOUTING DOWN. SOME OF US ARE TRYING TO SLEEP'. Yeah, I know I was also shouting, but I had every right to. My hangover, my headache. I own that fucker. No-one is going to take that away from me.

'Belle? What the hell?'
Oh hell no! It can't be? Probably isn't him. But there is only one person that ever called me that name. That bastard did a runner fifteen year ago though, and I haven't seen or heard from him since. Nope, can't possibly be him. Na ha, definitely not.
Maybe if I just take a quick peek to make sure. Maybe?

'RICHARD! GET OUT OF THAT BED NOW. YOU HAVE SOME EXPLAINING TO DO. LIKE WHY THE HELL YOU ARE FUCKING BELLE!'
Fuck! He did not just say that?
I sit up as quickly as humanly possible, considering the room was spinning. I fought back the urge to vomit again, as I squared my eyes at … yep … definitely him …James.

James and Richard are brothers. James is two years older than me and Richard, but the three of hung out together as kids. My parents and I moved next door to the Jarvis family, which consisted of their mother, the two brothers and a sister. The sister was only two years old then.
I found it difficult making new friends, but the Jarvis brothers took me under their wings. Me and Richard were six at the time and James eight. We became inseparable and we were known as the three musketeers.

THE SEXY FAKER

As we grew up, I started to have a crush on James. He was so different from his brother in many ways. Ricky and his sister looked like their mother. Blonde hair and blue eyes, whereas James had black hair and chocolate brown eyes and when he hit teenage years became dark and brooding, so I figured he must have taken after his father.

It was at my sixteenth birthday party when everything changed.

I was standing on the back porch getting some fresh air. The house was crammed with teenagers, mostly Ricky and James friends and some kids from the neighbourhood.

James came outside and stood next to me. He had his leather jacket on, that he always wore since getting it for his birthday the year before.

'Hey'.

'Hey. What's up James? Shouldn't you be inside with your girlfriend?' That last bit I couldn't help but say with a little disdain. Thankfully, James didn't seem to notice.

'I'd rather be out here with you Belle. You don't mind, do you?'

He was kidding right? Of course, I didn't mind. Hell, if I was brave enough and had the confidence, I would have jumped on him and kissed his face off. But, as much as I had a crush on my best friend, he didn't notice me in any other way but best friend. So, I kept my feelings to myself, because as young as I was, I knew that in my heart I loved him, and not just as a friend.

'Nope, of course not James. We're friends, aren't we? You can be with me anytime you want'.
I glanced a look at him and saw that he was smirking. I almost slapped my forehead, when I realised the innuendo.
Classy Annabelle, classy.

'I mean ... erm ... you know ... that erm'. Why was I so flustered?
James started laughing and turned to face me. Tucking a stray hair behind my ears.

'It's ok, don't worry. I knew what you meant'. His eyes went from mine to my lips, then back to my eyes again. He licked his lips. Oh god, was he going to kiss me? Is this the moment I have been longing for, in like, forever?
I lean forward and begin closing my eyes. My lips started to pucker, ready to feel his on mine.
Behind us the door slammed open, and the noise spilled outside. My eyes snap open. Great! Perfect timing.

'HEY BRO, COME ON, WE GOTTA GO'. One of James friends shouts to him.

'GIVE ME A MINUTE'. He called back.

'You should go. Your friends are waiting for you James'.
He stares at me. Almost thoughtfully, like I am a puzzle and he is trying to work me out. Then leans in and kisses my cheek.

'Your one special girl Belle. Don't let anyone tell you any different, ok?' He takes my hand and lifts it to his lips, kissing the top of my knuckles. It tickles, and I laugh at the ridiculousness of it.

'Don't ever stop laughing like that either. Do you hear me?'

I wave him off. 'Yeah ok'.
Little did I know, that was his goodbye. Looking back, I realised he was telling me that I would never see him again.

Now the cowardly bastard was back and shouting at his brother about fucking me?
Hell no!

'Now you look here, dip shit'. I spit out at him through gritted teeth, as I hurl my pillow at his head. He ducks, and it lands on the floor.

'Don't you dip shit me. You're the one in bed with my brother. So, I suggest ...'.

'Oh, you suggest do you? In case you haven't noticed, your brother and I are still dressed and have been drunkenly passed out on the bed since last night. And still would be if you hadn't come in here, like the dip shit you are, and start banging on doors and shouting. I think the people that live down the street heard you. So, forgive me if I am a little ... no, strike that ... a lot, pissed at you for barging in here and throwing accusations around. Especially when you don't even have the facts. Now, if you'll excuse me, I am outta here. Adios Ricky, catch you later. But you ...' I stab my finger in James chest now that I am close. 'You, can go back and crawl under that rock you came from'.

I try to make a dignified exit, but nope. Not me. Dignified is

definitely not my middle name.
The sea of bodies on the apartment floor look like they have doubled since last night. I go to step over one, but they move to turn over at the same time and my foot gets caught. Needless to say, I go flying through the air like a trapeze and face plant on the floor. But not before I crack my head on the corner of the coffee table on my way down. Perfect!

JAMES

I knew I shouldn't have left it so long to come back home, but the timing hadn't been right until now.
Seeing Belle in Richards bed had made my blood boil, even if I had no right to feel that way. It still felt like I had been stabbed in the heart. Because even though it had been fifteen years, I still loved the bones of her. My Belle. Only she isn't, and to be fair, she never was either. As much as I wanted her to be back then, I knew I wasn't good enough for her. Not after finding out what I did anyway. I knew she deserved someone better than me.
So, I left. To not only find what I was looking for but make myself worthy of her. Knowing that one day, I would come back for her.
It did pain me to know that she thought I had left her without a goodbye. That she wouldn't see or hear from me. The flip side to that was that I knew everything that had been happening in her life, because I had kept in touch with Richard. I had made him promise not to tell Belle though. I mean, he didn't know my address or anything like that, but he knew the whereabouts of where I was and what I had achieved over the years since leaving. He was my brother

after all. My mother was a different story all together. I loved her because she was my mother, but other than that, I had no interest in her knowing anything about me, nor me her. Not after her betrayal.

So, here I am, sitting in a hospital, in a cubicle with Belle lying on a gurney. Her eyes are still closed, which is a concern. After her fall, and with no help from Richard, I managed to get her downstairs and in to my car. My brother jumped in the back seat and we brought her to get checked out. I think she may have a concussion, she hit her head pretty hard. She has a nasty gash just above her eye and a friction burn just under her chin from the carpet.

Still my clumsy girl. If I wasn't so worried about her, I would have laughed at her escapade. But she hadn't woke up yet. Either that or she's pretending, so I'll go away and leave her alone. Not happening!

I look over at her again and sigh.

'Oh, god, are you still here'. She whimpered.

'Yes, I'm still here Belle. How are you feeling? You took a nasty bang to the head. You've had us worried'.

'Us? And I would feel much better if you weren't here'.

'Richard is outside. He still get's queasy when he see's blood'. I reached for her hand, but she snaps her hand away.

'What would you know what he does and doesn't like? You don't know anything about us. Just go away James'.

THE SEXY FAKER

'I can't do that'. I stand up and pace the bottom of the bed. The doctor comes through the curtain and proceed to ask what happened before examining her.

'Well, you don't need stitches, so that's good. But you say you're still feeling dizzy? So, it seems you may have mild concussion. So, bed rest and do you have someone who can wake you every couple of hours for today and tonight?'.

'No'.

'Yes'.

I said yes at the same time as Belle said no. The doctor looked from me to Belle then back to me again.

'I'll be fine doctor. I can get one of my friends to stay over and take care of me'. Yeah, I know for a fact she had no friends. Her best friend was Richard, and I know he couldn't stay with her because he had work tonight.

'I can take care of her Doctor. It's not a problem'. The doctor left us alone, while Belle gave me the death stare.

'You're staring'. I inform her.

'What? No, I'm not. Why are you here James? No-one see's you in almost fifteen years, then you walk in to Ricky's apartment and start throwing your weight around. Making absurd accusations'.

'Accusations? I found you in bed together Belle'. I throw back at her.

'Oh my god! We were fully clothed, or are you blind as well as stupid?' She rolled her eyes at me.

THE SEXY FAKER

'You know what? I didn't come back for this'. I spit out.

'Then go. I never asked you to sit here with me'. She bit back.

I throw my hands up in the air. 'Still the stubborn, annoying, frustrating girl I left behind, I see'.

'Still the arrogant, egotistical bastard who left, I see'. She says, narrowing her eyes.

'You know what …'.

'What?'
We stare at each other, for mere seconds, but it felt more like minutes.

I sigh. 'Never mind'. I turn to leave.

'Fine'. She spits out.

'Fine'. I don't even look back at her. I pull the curtain open wide and leave.

JAMES

I find Richard in the waiting area and sit down beside him, letting out a deep breath. I drop my head forward, resting my elbows on my knees.

'How is she doing?'

'It's Belle, how do you think she's doing?' I couldn't help but laugh. Richard chuckled too, because even after all these years, we both knew what Belle was like.

'You know we didn't sleep together, right? I mean, me and Annabelle have never had sex. She's like a sister to me bro, besides ...'. He pauses and scratches his chin.

'Besides what Richard? Just spit it out, I know you are dying to enthral me with some wisdom'.

'I would never step on your toes'.
I sit up, looking at him incredulously. 'I have no idea what you are talking about'.

'Look Jimmy, I ...'. I hold my hand up, stopping him mid-sentence.

'Don't call me that, you know very well I hate it'.

'Fine. James. I know you have a thing for her. You have always had a thing for her, since we were kids. I also know you never acted on it because she was your best friend'.

'Is my best friend Richard. She will always be my best friend'.

'Yeah, somehow, I don't think that is so anymore, not since you left anyway. You kind of broke her heart a little, leaving without saying goodbye. Don't get me wrong, she pretended she was fine and tried to act all "I don't really care that he's gone" I would see the look on her face, when she thought no-one was looking. But I knew, I saw she was hurting'.

'Fuck! I figured she would miss me and be somewhat hurt. I thought that maybe in time she'd get over it and move on. Shit! Do you think she will forgive me, so we can be at least be friends again? I missed her and the last thing I want to do is hurt her again'.

'Depends bro. Will have to be something pretty selfless to win her round. Does she know that you're back for good?'

'No, I haven't said anything yet. Now that I am back though, I can take my time to gain her trust again'.

'So, what's the plan?'

'Actually, the plan has fallen right in to my lap. The doctor said she can't be left alone today and tonight. She has a mild concussion, so has to be kept an eye on. You're working tonight right?'

'Yeah, why?' He looked at me suspiciously.

'Because you won't be available to keep an eye on her. But I can'.

'Annabelle will never go for it'. Richard slapped him on his back, laughing and shaking his head.

'She won't have a choice. Once I get her back to my apartment, I will treat her like a queen. Spoil her and pamper her, until she is well again. Then she will see just how much I Lo … I mean care about her. She won't be able to not trust me again after that and then we will be friends again'.

'Wow. That is some plan you have formulated. Not sure it will work, but I wish you good luck with it. I'll go pop and see her, see how she's doing. Hopefully the doctor will let her home now. She has a hatred for hospitals since her car accident. She had a broken leg, but you'd think she had been given open heart surgery the way she moaned about it'. Ricky waved his hand at me as I watched him walk down the corridor.

I thought back to the night eight years ago, when Richard had called me to tell me that Belle had been involved in a car accident. I had almost jumped on a plane to come back here, but my brother had reassured me she was ok. She had only sustained a broken leg and a few bruises and scratches. I had wanted to come back then, to be with her, but knew the timing wasn't right.

I had worked too damn hard now to have everything fall apart before it had begun. My past no longer dominated my life or my decisions anymore. I only hoped that I could make it up to Belle. I also knew it wasn't going to be easy, but I was definitely up for the challenge.

I was still sitting in the waiting room, when Richard and Belle came walking down the corridor. She didn't look very pleased to see me at all. Nothing new there then.
Richard started speaking as they approached me.
'So, Annabelle and I have been talking and it seems she can't be left on her own until tomorrow, that is, if she has no more effects from the concussion. So, I kind have allocated you Ji ... I mean, James, as her carer'.
I could see the look of disdain on her face. She couldn't even look at me. Her eyes went everywhere but me.

I clear my throat. 'Well, then I guess we should get going home then'.
Her snaps around to me. 'Where? Because there is no way I am going home with you. If I have to be subjected to this farce, then I will do so in the comfort of my own home, thank you very much'.
I hold up my hands in defeat. 'Of course Belle, whatever you want. However, I will need to stop by my place to pick up a few things, I ...'.

'What? What do you mean, your place? You have a place? Here?'. The shocked expression on her face was priceless.

'Yes, Belle, I have a place ... here. Come on, and if you behave yourself, I may show you around'.
She scoffed. 'Yeah, no thanks. I'll pass. Richard can drive me home and you can come by later'.

THE SEXY FAKER

'Sorry chick, but I have to get ready for work, so no time to drop you off'. Belle rolled her eyes at him.

'Fine!' She spun on heel and called over her shoulder. 'Are you coming then, or what?'

'You better hustle bro. Annabelle waits for no-one'.

'Yeah, no kidding. I'll call you tomorrow'.
I quickened my step to catch up with her. Boy, could she walk fast, even with a concussion.
He was going to have his work cut out with her.

ANNABELLE

This can not be my life right now. The prodigal turns up after fifteen years and my life gets thrown in to turmoil.
I have had to ring in sick to work, because of this stupid concussion. Which I most certainly blame James for. If he hadn't have come back I would never have tripped over Tina's stupid ass and face planted on the floor. Nor would I now be sporting a questionable carpet burn under my chin! Now, I have to spend more time with the scarlet pimpernel himself. Argh! This cannot be my life!
For the last ten minutes he has be perusing my apartment, like someone who is assessing the square footage for purchase.
Oh, hell no! He did not just wipe his finger across my book shelf!
'Hey, I think I … erm … I'm going to go lie down for a bit. You know where the kitchen is now, so make yourself a coffee or something'.
He turns to face, putting his hands in his jean pockets.
'How about I make us something to eat. You must be hungry by now?'
Urgh! Why is he being so damn nice to me. All I have done

since he walked in to Ricky's bedroom is be a bitch to him.
'I'm not really that hungry'. Just then my tummy rumbled.
Traitor!
'Why don't I make us something to eat while you freshen up.
Then you can go rest for a bit. I'll wake you in say what ...two
hours? Then we can talk. We have a lot to discuss, a lot of
catching up to do'.

'Ok'. Was all I could come up with. Jesus Annabelle, when the
hell did you not have anything to say, about anything?
I quickly freshened up and went back in to the living room.
James was nowhere to be seen. He must be in the kitchen.
Nope.
Where the hell was he. I walked through my apartment but
couldn't find him anywhere.
What the hell! Have I been dreaming everything that has
happened since this morning? Ok, admittedly, I generally
dream about James. Have done for the last fifteen years, and
last night was no exception. But to dream it while still been
awake! Wow, that is a new low, even for me.
I headed towards my bedroom. A nice hot bubble bath will
do the trick. But as I neared, I could hear singing coming from
inside. I peeked around the door, no-one was in the
bedroom. I could see steam billowing from the bathroom
door though. Damn it! He's in there and in my shower by the
sounds of it. I was about to turn around and head back to the
living room. Unfortunately, years of speculation about how
he looked was too much to deny myself. So, I inched my way
in the room and towards the bathroom door, that was

slightly ajar.
I could see his naked reflection in the mirror. He was soaped up and was bending down, running his hands up and down his thick muscular calves. Still singing some Sinatra song. Wow! His body was that of a Greek god, no doubt about it.
I don't know if it was from the heat and steam of the shower or I was literally sweating from the heat of his body. But damn, I was feeling my temperature rise.
I licked my lips, when I saw the trails of water dripping down the contour of his body. He was standing now, and I could see his toned abs and pecs.
Fucking hell! I think my lady bits have just started a party. It certainly felt like a pool party down there.
FUCK ME!

'EXCUSE ME?'

Shit! Did I say that out loud?

'YES, YOU DID SAY IT OUT LOUD. ARE YOU ENJOYING THE SHOW? LIKE SOMETHING YOU SEE BELLE?'
Why was I stepping further in to the bathroom instead of apologising and leaving? Because I'm an idiot that is why. Now he is turning the shower off and stepping out, grabbing the towel off the rail and rubbing it all over his body.
Holy fucking hell!
'You're thinking aloud again Belle. Do you make a habit of that? Because I am sure it will get you in to ... trouble'.

'What? I mean ... no, I don't generally think aloud. It's just that you ... I mean ... you ... ahh, fuck it, who am I kidding.

THE SEXY FAKER

You've gotten hot James. When did that happen? Wait, no, don't answer that. I think I had better leave now'. I grip the door handle to pull it shut on my way out when he says my name.

'Belle'. It was barely a whisper. But I heard it and turned back around to face him. His eyes had darkened and were slightly hooded with desire. I gulped.

'Yes, James?'

'I Can't wait to hear you say those words again to me'.
Huh?

'Words? What words?'

He took a tentative step towards me and I clutched the door handle as if my life depended on it. Hell, it was the only thing keeping upright at the moment.

'Fuck me and yes. Because one day Belle you will beg me to fuck you and I will have you saying yes, over and over again. I will make you come so hard, you'll forget your own name'.

'Don't count on it'. I said and left him standing there.
CRAP!

Yeah ok, I was lying to myself, because I knew he could make me do those things without even trying. But I could not, would not, give in to him and his seductions. I will not allow myself to be hurt by him ever again. He left once and didn't look back. God knows why he's here now or for how long, but I refuse to be drawn in to his fickle life.

Not this time.

JAMES

I watched her face contort in to different expressions. I could see the cog working in her brain. I knew she had a million questions she wanted to ask me. She just didn't know where to start.
We continued to eat in silence instead. After what seemed an age, she placed her fork down and she finally spoke.
'Where have you been James?'
Well, how the hell am I supposed to answer that direct question? I mean, I knew it was coming, but I figured she would ease in to it. I guess I forgot how much of a straight to the point girl she was ... is.
I clear my throat. 'I've been living in the states. L.A to be precise'.

'Wow! I mean ... wow. I don't know what to say about that'.
She picks up her fork and starts to eat again.
Me on the other hand, is sitting on tenterhooks, waiting for the next question.
'So, what is it you do over there?'

'I sell real estate, and before you ask, yes I love it. I actually started the company myself, when I got fed up of doing all the grunt work for someone else, then they would take the credit for all the hard work I had done. It was a no brainer really. Took me five years to bring the company from nothing to where it is now. We are one of the top three company's clients come to when they want to purchase high end, top quality homes'.

'Again, wow. I can't believe you are so successful'.
I quirk a brow at her.
'Sorry, that didn't come out right. I mean, I can believe it, I always knew you would make something of yourself. That you would be somebody'.

'Yeah?'

'Yeah'. She sighs and let's her fork clatter on the plate.
'What happened James? Why did you leave?'
I wipe my mouth with the napkin and place it on my plate. Turning to face her, I look in to her eyes and search her face. Was I ready to tell her my deepest, darkest secret about why I had to leave? No, I wasn't. Not until I could gain her trust back.
'I would rather not talk about that right now. When the time is right, I will tell you everything. I promise'.

'Then at least tell me why you came back. You owe me that much James'.
I push my chair back and hold my hand out for her.
'If we are going to have this discussion, let us get comfortable, maybe have a glass of wine. Believe me when I say, by the time I have finished, you are going to need a

drink'.

She stares at my hand, then looks up at me cautiously. I see her gulp and the corner of her eye twitches.

'Is what you are about to tell me that bad James?'

'Well, not so much what I am about to tell you, but maybe what I have to suggest afterwards. Don't worry though, you have plenty of time to think it over and let me know what you decide'.

The look now on her face was unreadable. I used to be able to know exactly what she was thinking, just like earlier. It seems, over the years, she has developed a skill of dead panning.

After pouring us both a glass of wine, we took a seat on her sofa.

'Ok James, I'm ready, so spill'.

I take a deep breath and begin. 'First, I want you to know that I am back for good. I have moved my office here. My main offices will remain in L.A of course, but from now on I will be working from here'.

'So, you've moved back home, permanently?'

'Yes, I have. L.A is great, don't get me wrong, but I needed a change of pace. I needed to be around … genuine people again. Everyone there is fake, and I couldn't trust anyone. No-one there matters'.

I watch her contemplating my words. She studies my face to see if I am telling her the truth.

'What about your erm … wife? Girlfriend? Are they willing to up sticks and move too?'

THE SEXY FAKER

I chuckled, because I knew she was fishing. It was written on her face. And as much as I wanted to tell her the truth, I also needed to know if she felt anything for me. If she would be jealous. So instead I choose to give her a vague answer. 'Where I go they go, it's not really up for discussion'.

'Huh? So, you just tell your … your … you know, never mind what they think or what they might want to do? Wow, that is just so … arrogant and chauvinistic of you James. I mean, how could you be such a …'.

I hold my hand up, stopping her from saying another word she will regret. I couldn't lie anymore, not if I want her to go through with my plan any way.

'Ok, before you finish that sentence and embarrass yourself, I think you misunderstood what I meant Belle. I don't have a wife, or fiancée or girlfriend for that matter, I'm single. What I was saying is that if I had a woman in my life, if she really loved me then she would go wherever I was going. And before you say anything, I was going to add, that if the roles were reversed, then I would go where she was too. Now, does that change your opinion of me being a sexist pig?' I raise a brow.

'Does it really matter what I think James? Your life has nothing to do with me. Not since you left anyway'. She took a sip of her wine, peering at me over the rim.

'Yes, it matters what you think. It has always mattered to me what you think Belle'. I take the glass from hand and place it down on the coffee table. Then hold her hand in mine. She tries to pull it back, but I squeeze tight, so she can't.

'James, what are you doing?' she whispers. Her eyes becoming hooded, which only sends a pulse to my cock. My pants are getting tighter by the minute.
'I'm holding your hand'.
She searches my face. I know exactly what she is looking for. I lean forward and gently, softly kiss her. My lips brushing, almost a whisper on her lips. A kiss I should have given her when I was eighteen. When I knew she wanted me to before we were interrupted on the night I left. And not kissing her was my only other regret I had in my life, other than leaving her.
She put's her hand on my chest and gently pushes me back, ending the kiss abruptly. She touches her lips lightly with her forefinger.
'If you think you can come back here after all these years and just … just …kiss me. Then you can think again'.

'Belle, I am so sorry. Forgive me, that wasn't my intention at all'. I say, pulling back from her.
'I think you should go James'. Belle stands up and walks towards the window, her back to me.
I look up at the ceiling and take a deep breath. This is not how I wanted this to go. But no way was I letting her push me away now. I left her once and I wasn't doing again.
'I'm not going anywhere Belle. Remember, you need to be chaperoned until morning. So, I am afraid you are stuck with me and I promise you, you have nothing to worry about. I don't bite, well, not if you don't want me to'.

THE SEXY FAKER

She spun round so fast, I thought she might get whiplash. 'What did you just say to me?'

'I said ... never mind. Look, the point is I am here to make sure you are ok, like the doctor said. Nothing more, so stop worrying. Now, if you've finished eating, maybe you should go lie down for a bit and I'll come check on you in a few hours. Unless you would like to have a soak first, I could run you a bath if you'd like?'

'Thanks, but I am more than capable of running myself a bath'. She left me glaring after her back.
Jesus! When did she become so goddam infuriating? I knew when I left, that she would be hurt by it. But I never realised she would still be hurting or how much. Maybe I was naïve to think she would have forgotten about me and moved on. Maybe she did have feelings more than friendship for me back then. Maybe she still had those feelings. Or maybe, it is just my wishful thinking. Fuck!
I need more time to convince her that she can trust me, that I am not going anywhere. I am here to stay. Unfortunately, thanks to my board members, I didn't have the luxury of time. They have given me one month to settle my shit down or they will boot me out of my own company. A company that I built up from nothing, and I was damned if I was going to let them kick me to the curb.
All I had to do was prove to them that I was no longer the man whore I had apparently been dubbed in L.A. "The real estate Lothario" was what one magazine had headlined with. I couldn't deny it either, much to my chagrin! There were

pictures of me and a different woman on my arm every week, and it was just the way I liked it. That is until I met the delusional bitch that was Davina Boothright. Model and down right obsessive. She was like a leech, clinging on to me for dear life, which was my own fault, because I went on more than one date with her. So, she assumed that meant I wanted more than just a one and done with her. The press hadn't helped either. Speculating about have I finally found the one. Was I settling down at last. That shit alone was reason enough for me to leave L.A.

So, the board had made it very clear, shape up or ship out. The only problem with that was, none of the women I had dalliances with were up to the job. None of them challenged me mentally or physically. Hell, I couldn't even have decent conversation with most of them, not that it mattered, we both knew that it was only about dinner and sex. As far as I was concerned, I didn't want to spend the rest of my life with someone I didn't love. There was only one woman that title went to. For she was the only one I had ever loved and still do. I just needed to convince her, for my plan to work, and my hope was that in time she would fall in love with me too.

Belle. The only one I could see my future with.

THE SEXY FAKER

ANNABELLE

Some fucker was shaking me to death. Whoever it is I will punch them in the throat, if they don't stop right now. I swing my arm out from under the cover, but only hit air. I groan and roll over on to my back, slinging my arm over my eyes. 'Whoever you are, please go fuck yourself and leave me alone'.

'Belle, wake up honey'. James drawl makes me groan again.

'For the love of god James, leave me alone. This is the third time you have woke me up in as many minutes. Go away. Don't you have anything better to do with your time?'

'Belle, it's morning, and the last time I woke you up was four hours ago. I've made you some breakfast. Come on get up, you need to eat and then shower. Richard is on his way over'.

'What time is it?' I say, squinting up at James. Why did he have to be so damn good looking, especially dressed in a black suit and crisp white shirt, sporting a burgundy silk tie. He checks his watch. 'Ten thirty. Like I said Rich ...'. The doorbell buzzer shut's him up. 'That's probably Richard now. Get out of bed, now Belle'.

THE SEXY FAKER

I sat up straight then, when I realised he said Ricky was here. Did that mean he was leaving now? Where was he going? I thought he had told he was staying here to take care of me? Why am I suddenly freaking out about him going? Why did I care? For fucks sakes!
I heard voices in the other room. They were talking too quiet for me to hear. I climbed out of bed and padded across to the bedroom door, putting my ear against it.
'I think she's ok now Richard. Why you felt the need to come here I don't know'.

'Because she is my best friend in case you've forgotten. Just because you spent the night here looking after her, doesn't mean she has forgiven you. I still don't get why you couldn't have told her, instead of having her think you didn't care about her'.

'Like I have told you over the years Richard, I did it because I did care about her. I still do as you well know'.

'Are you going to tell her everything now you are back for good?'

'In time. Right now, I have to gain her trust again before I tell her anything'.

'How do you suppose to do that?'

'I have something up my sleeve. I just hope it all goes to plan because if not, I will not only lose Belle, but I will lose my company too'.

'What? Tell me everything James'.

THE SEXY FAKER

'Well, I ...'.
Damn, they must have moved to the living room because I couldn't hear anymore. But what the fuck! Ricky knew where James was all this time? Why would he keep that from me? Me and him will definitely be having words once James has left. And what the hell is James planning that will make him gain my trust?
I heard footsteps coming down the hall towards my room. Shit! I rushed in to the En-suite and turned on the shower. Undressing, I jumped in and started washing myself. I heard a light tap on the bathroom door.
'Hey Annabelle, it's Ricky. Are you ok in there? James as just left, so I'm here to keep you company'.

'YEAH, I'M GOOD RICKY. YOU DON'T HAVE TO STAY THOUGH'.

'JAMES SAID I WASN'T TO LEAVE YOU ALONE. NOT UNTIL HE COMES BACK ANYWAY'.

Come back? Why the hell would he come back here? Oh, hell no! I touched my lips again, like I had done a million times since he kissed me last night. I could still taste him on me when I licked my lips. It wasn't the passionate kiss that I had craved from him fifteen years ago. No, it was much better. Softer, gentle, like it meant something. I shook my head because I knew that wasn't true. He didn't feel anything for me. I knew it then and I know it now.
I turned the shower and grabbed a towel, wrapping it around me and slinging the door open. Ricky was sat on the edge of my bed, looking up at me when I entered the bedroom.

Why was he looking at me like that? He's been in my bedroom hundreds of times and seen me with just a towel around me, but he has never looked at me like the way he is now. There is lust in his eyes. What the hell!

'Ricky, you know you don't need to be here right? I'm ok now'. I moved around the bedroom, collecting my clothes to take back in to the bathroom. No way was I getting dressed in front of him.

'Annabelle ...'. He jumped up and approached me, standing within an inch of my face. I could feel his minty breath on my lips. One of his hands rests on my hip, while the other he brings up to my cheek, cupping it.

'Ricky, what are you doing?' I whisper, closing my eyes, because even though he's my best friend, he is still a man, and it has been so long since a man has touched me.

'I don't know. I just felt the need to touch you. You're my best friend and I have never crossed this line with you but ... I guess with James coming back, I've realised I have feelings for you. I think, more than best friend feelings ... can I kiss you Annabelle'. He brushed his lips against my cheek.

What was I doing? Should I let him kiss me, and see if there are any feelings there? Would I lose my best friend if I rejected him? The one thing I did know for sure, was that I was still hung up on James. Damn him for coming back now and mixing my head up.

I shook my head. I couldn't do this. Not when all I can think about is James.

'Ricky, I'm sorry. I can't do this, you're my best friend and I love you, just not in that way. Please don't stop being my

THE SEXY FAKER

friend though, I couldn't bare it if that happened'. I was pleading with him now.

'Annabelle, I am so sorry. Please forgive me'. His eyes widen as he steps away from me. 'I don't know what came over me. I should go. Tell James I had a work thing or something'. Then he left. Me standing there as confused as ever.

JAMES

I hated having to leave Belle so soon this morning, but I had to get back to my place for a face time conference call from the board of directors. This was my last chance to appease them and make sure they wouldn't kick me out of my own company.

All I had to do was make a convincing argument to Belle now, to go along with my plan. A plan I had intended to discuss with her last night, but that had all gone tits up, when I had allowed myself to lose control and kissed her. I was still a little puzzled as to why she pushed me away. I had thought it was what she had wanted, I had seen it in her eyes. The way she stared at my lips, while she licked hers. I have had enough experience to know when a woman wants me and when she doesn't, and I was damn sure Belle wanted me last night.

My mistake was to jump in too soon. She wasn't ready yet for me to seduce her, like she wasn't ready fifteen years ago. Leaving was the only option I had at that time. I had important shit going on in my life back then that needed sorting out. Dragging Belle and her family into it was not an option. So, I left the one good thing I had in my life. The only

THE SEXY FAKER

girl I have ever loved, I left behind in the hopes she would move on and find someone who was worthy of her.
I'm so glad she didn't though. Yeah, that's the selfish bastard in me. Knowing that every relationship she had attempted was shit. Richard always updated me on the guys she dated. Some had been ok, and some had been total scumbags who had treated her like she was nothing. I used to blame myself for a while, that if I hadn't of left, I would have been around to stop her dating dickheads. But then, I would have only gotten jealous when she dated good guys.
In my mind, all the guys struck out because she was in love with me and couldn't forget me. That she was waiting for me. Guess I was wrong.

Trevor Oxford, the head of the board was the proverbial thorn in my side! It was him who had persuaded the others to this ridiculous ultimatum, for me to "settle down".

'So, James do you have good news for us? It has been a month now after all'.

I smiled sheepishly and rubbed the back of my neck. I hated lying to them when I hadn't had a chance to speak to Belle properly yet. I had to give them something for now though to keep them on side.

'I'll say, well believe it or not, I actually bumped in to an old girlfriend I used to date when I was eighteen. We kind of caught up and realised we still loved each other. So, yeah we're back together'.

Trevor clapped his hands together. 'That is fantastic news James, absolutely fantastic. So, when is the big day? Soon I hope. Hey, maybe a summer wedding, that would be perfect. I know Margie is looking forward to buying a new hat. Oh, this is perfect, perfect my boy. Congratulations'.
I almost choked. 'Trevor, I … erm … I haven't asked her yet'.

'What?!

SHIT! Think James, think.
'Oh, I mean tonight! Yeah, I will be asking her tonight. We're going to dinner, somewhere romantic. You know, candles, roses and all that. So, yeah tonight'. Fuck is it hot in here or is it me. Because I am sweating cobs right now, and I am sure this suit has shrunk while I have been sitting here.

'You haven't told us the lucky ladies name James'.

'It's Belle'.

'Oh, what a beautiful name. Well, I am just so pleased you finally came to your senses. Right then, we will see you in two weeks at the opening of the new offices'.

'Of course, see you then'. The screen on my laptop went black.
Fuck! Now all I had to do was convince Belle to go along with my plan, which will then, hopefully, make her fall in love with me. Because not being with her anymore was not an option. My phone rang then, bringing me out of my daze. Richard's

timing was always impeccable.
'What is it Richard?'

'I think you need to get back here. I did ... erm ... something. I think she might be pissed at me or upset. Never can tell with her'.

'What the hell did you do?'

'I may have come on to her. Now before you start, I was just laying the ground work for you. You know, seeing how she would react to me, cause if she had fallen in to my arms then at least you would know she didn't still have any more feelings for you. I was just trying to help'.
Oh for fucks sake! I seriously think my brother has a screw loose. Maybe he was dropped on his head or something as a baby. He was always doing stupid shit when we were kids and it was always me that had to bail him out.
Wait! Did he say she might have feelings for me, still?
'What the hell is wrong with you? Why would you do something like that? And stop with all that feelings shit will you, your starting to give me hives!' Hopefully that will throw him off until I have a chance to speak to Belle first.

'Fine, but you still need to get back to her place, she practically threw me out, saying she was ok now'.
I let out an exasperated breath. 'Luckily I have just finished up here. I'll go check on her and see you later'. I hung the phone before he could reply.
That brother of mine is going to be the death of me one of these days!

THE SEXY FAKER

I am about to leave my apartment when my phone buzzes again. Jesus! If that is Richard again ...
I look at the caller I.D, an L.A dialling code. Fucking Davina! What the hell does she want now? I thought I had made myself perfectly clear before I left there.
'What do you want Davina?'

'Darling, do you have to be so cold with me?'

'I don't have time for any of your bull shit, so just spit it out'.

'I miss you James. When are you coming home?'
I sigh, because I had already told her we were through, when I caught her fucking one of my associates in his office. Lucky for me huh, that I had forgotten something and had to head back in to work. His office was next to mine, and I heard noises when I passed by his door, which was ajar. Glad I was a nosy fucker and looked in too, because I would have never had known she was a cheating bitch otherwise. Not that I really cared that things were over between us. I just didn't like that she fucked someone else behind my back. They were welcome to each other.
So, yet another reason why I left L.A and came back home. To get away from that conniving cow, who has constantly blown up my phone ever since.
Didn't love her, hell I wasn't even sure that I had liked her that much to be honest. She was a decent fuck and had all the right connections. She was a model and also ten years younger than me too, which I suppose didn't help.
'I am home Davina. Like I told you before I left L.A, there is no

us anymore. Not after you fucked someone else. Stop calling me, stop texting me and leave me the fuck alone'.

'James, please. I have told you how sorry I am. Forgive me already, so we can move on. Don't you remember how good I make you feel? When I slide my tongue down your hard, throbbing cock. When I …'.

'STOP! For gods sake woman, have some dignity. You're embarrassing yourself. Now, I shall say this for the last time Davina. Leave. Me. Alone. Otherwise I will be forced to speak to my lawyer. Now, do yourself and me a favour, lose my fucking number'. I pressed the end button and took a deep breath. When she was spouting on about how good she made me feel, it made me feel only one thing. Sick to my stomach. Don't get me wrong, yes, she could make me hard and yes, she could make me come. But it would take forever because I just wasn't that in to it. Sex was sex to me. I wasn't a selfish lover by any means, I always made sure the woman I was with received pleasure upon pleasure before I took mine. It was just that, Davina wanted more than I could give her, and to me, that was a turn off.

There was only one woman I would and wanted to ever give my full self to, and that was Belle. She is the one and only woman who I left my heart in her pocket to find.

I just hope she finds it soon.

ANNABELLE

Could this day get any worse! First, I had to wake up to that asshole James in my face. Then Ricky declaring his undying love. I locked myself out of my apartment, because I was in such a hurry to get in to work this afternoon, I forgot to pick up my keys off the table by the side of the door when I left! My car wouldn't start, so I had to call for a taxi that wouldn't be able to pick me up for thirty minutes, and thanks to good old British weather, it was raining hard and I didn't have my umbrella.
When I eventually arrived at work at lunch time and looking like a drowned rat, everyone, and I mean everyone! Had already gone out to lunch. So, I had come in to my office, only to be faced with the one person I wished had also gone to lunch. The office pervert, Kent Draxton!
'Why are you sat in my chair Kent?'

'Why are you late in to the office Annabelle and why didn't you come in to work yesterday? Hangover from hell was it?' The bastard smirked. I hated the slimy sleaze ball and his smirking ugly Chewbacca face.
Unfortunately he was also one of the partners of the law firm

THE SEXY FAKER

I worked for. Bilton, Dennis & Draxton.

'I had a bit of an accident yesterday and the doctor at the hospital told me I had a mild concussion. So, I had to take the day off work and be chaperoned until this morning to make sure I was ok, that there were no after effects from my head injury. Now, will you please remove yourself from my chair, so I can get to work?' I pointed to the scab that had now formed above my eye, and moved around my desk, making sure I was still two arm's length away from him.

'Hmm ... and how did you get that carpet burn? Was this a sexual accident Annabelle? Were you on your knees getting fucked from behind and it was that rough, you ended up with injuries?'

Jesus Christ, I think I just threw up in my mouth. The guy was beyond gross, and it wasn't the first time he had made lude comments to me.

I roll my eyes at him. 'Kent, I would like to get some work done now please. Can you move?'

Sure enough, he slinked out of my chair and headed in my direction, but I was too quick and went around the desk in the opposite direction, sitting down in my chair.

Instead of leaving the weasel came back around and stood in front of me, peering down at me with his beady little eyes.

'Why don't you just answer the question, and then maybe ...'. He leaned down, gripping the arm rests, blocking me. His face only centimetres away from mine. '... we can have some fun of our own. I know you want me, I see the way you look at me when you think I am not watching. But I see it, I see you. You're sexy and I know my cock would make you feel so good, when I am pounding you hard in that tight little pussy of yours. You'll be screaming my name over and over, begging me not to stop and I ... ARRGH!'

I gasped, because I had no idea what the hell was happening, other than Kent going flying to the other side of the room. I stood up and watched him hit the wall and drop to the floor with a thud.

It wasn't until I heard his voice, that I realised James was in the room too. I turned to face him, noticing he was actually stood right next to me. I blinked at him, trying to comprehend what the hell he was doing in my office.

He was still talking to me, though I wasn't quite hearing what he was saying to me. Then I heard Kent shouting about suing someone and calling the police for assault.

'YOU BROKE MY FUCKING NOSE. YOU'LL PAY FOR THIS'. Kent was now pointing a finger at James while holding his bleeding nose with his other hand.

I snapped out of my daze then, because hell no, was Kent going after James.

'SHUT UP KENT. IF YOU HAD'NT BEEN SEXUALLY HARRASSING ME THEN JAMES WOULDN'T HAVE HAD TO PULL YOU OFF ME. I'M SURE THE OTHER PARTNERS WILL JUST LOVE TO HEAR ABOUT THIS, ESPECIALLY SINCE I NOW HAVE A WITNESS. SO, FUCK OFF BACK TO YOUR OWN OFFICE AND LEAVE ME TO GET ON WITH MY OWN WORK'.

Kent mumbled something as he scuttled passed us and out the door.

I slumped back in to my chair, trying to catch my breath I hadn't realised I was holding.

THE SEXY FAKER

I looked up at James then, who was standing in front of me, towering over me. He reached down and tucked some loose hair behind my ear.

'Are you ok Belle?' The concern in his voice shocked me for some reason.

Staring up at him, I nodded. 'Yeah, thanks for that. What are you doing here anyway?'

'Richard called me and told me what happened. He said I needed to get back to your place, but I got there and you weren't in, obviously. One of your neighbours said you had probably gone to work, so here I am'. He perched himself on the edge of my desk.

We stared at each other for some time and it was starting to become an uncomfortable silence.

I cleared my throat. 'Any way, I should get back to work. Thanks for stopping by and for earlier with Kent'.

He narrowed his eyes at me. 'Does that scumbag put his hands on you often Belle?'

I drop my shoulders and let out a sigh. 'He's never put his hands on me before. He's just a creep and says inappropriate shit to all the women who work here. He's also one of the partners, so it's difficult for anyone to report him. Don't get me wrong, the other partners are cool, and nothing like Kent. But I have a feeling they would have his back over some stupid woman making accusations with no proof'.

James shook his head. A look of disappointment on his face. 'Belle, the one thing you are not, is stupid. You are a strong, beautiful, independent woman and I can't believe you would let him get away with what he's been doing. This isn't the Belle I know. You would have fought tooth and nail for anything when we were kids. Remember when Mr Peterson wanted to fill in that pond on his land, and you were so worried about the pond life in it that would die. You wrote out a petition and went around all the neighbours to get signatures. Then you made a pack lunch and had Richard and I follow you down to that damned pond and stage a sit-down protest. What happened to that girl Belle? Why aren't you fighting?'

'Because I am not a kid anymore and this is more serious that a stupid pond and pond life James. Now, could you please leave, I have work to do'. I looked away from him then and grabbed a file off the top of a stack on my desk.
James blew out a long breath and let his head drop, he rubbed the palm of his hands over his muscular thighs. Yeah, that's right, I said muscular thighs because you can't miss them when they're pulling his trousers taught like that.
The bulge in is trouser I couldn't miss either and he wasn't even hard. God help the woman who had to tackle that thing. And I couldn't help licking my lips and wishing I could be that woman. Wow, lady bits sure were doing a jig down there, I had to cross my legs when I felt myself start to throb.
I looked up when James cleared his throat. He had a bemused expression.
'See something you like?' He quirked a brow.

'What?' Jesus, was I flustered?

'I asked if you saw something you liked. You were staring at my dick'.

'I was doing no such thing'. I spluttered.

'I think you'll find you were. I'll see you tonight'. He laughed then stood up.

'Huh? Tonight, why will you see me tonight?'

'I'm taking you to dinner, so be ready for seven thirty when I pick you up'.

I was too stunned to speak and when I finally snapped out of it, he was gone.

Shit! Dinner? I didn't want to go to dinner with the deserter!

JAMES

I was on my way to pick Belle up for dinner. It had taken me forever to decide what to wear and I never take that long, ever. I was also nervous for some reason. What I had to be nervous about, I don't know. I had known her all my life, so why all of a sudden was my palms sweaty and my tie felt like it was choking me. Why I even put a tie on is beyond me! I shake my head at my own idiocy and start to loosen my tie and remove it. I unbutton the top three buttons of my black dress shirt and pull it out from my grey trousers.
When I pull up outside Belle's building I roll my sleeves up, making me look and feel more casual than I did before I left. I feel a little more relaxed, though I still have some butterflies, I haven't spoken to her since this afternoon at her office, so I have no idea if she will even go out with me tonight.
I make my way inside and up to her apartment. Knocking twice on her door, I wait. Rubbing my sweaty palms down my trousers. What the hell is wrong with me? Get it together James for fucks sake!

THE SEXY FAKER

The door swings open and a blonde goddess appears before me. She was wearing a tight red dress that accentuated her curvy hips and perfectly pert round breasts. Her long blonde hair was loose and flowing around her shoulders and her bright blue eyes appeared bluer thanks to the smoky eye make-up. She had moderate heels on, but they still made her toned legs look longer. Fucking gorgeous.

'Fuck Belle, you look … wow … you look fucking speechless beautiful. Are you ready to go?'

'You look good too James. Where are we going?' she picked a clutch up from the table beside the door, before pulling the door closed and locking it. We walked side by side to the elevator. I didn't dare risk touching her because I didn't think I would be able to stop. Because right now all I could think about was having those gorgeous legs of hers wrapped around my waist while I pumped my cock in to her. Dammit! At this rate I'll have to go to the men's toilets at the restaurant and knock one out, just to get some release! I can already feel my trousers getting tighter, thank god I pulled my shirt out and was covering what would be considered, embarrassing.

'James?'

I turn to see the questioning look on Belle's face.

'What?'

'I asked you where we were going'.

'Oh, right. Romeo's, I booked us a table. I know you love Italian food'.

'Wow, how the hell did you manage that? That place as a waiting list three month ahead of time'.

'I have my methods'. I gave her my widest smile and she smiled back. Well, that is a good start. Let's hope I can keep that smile on her face for the rest of the evening.

We arrived at Romeo's twenty minutes early. The hostess pointed us in the direction of the bar until out table was ready.
'What would you like to drink?'
Belle studied the drinks menu before opting for a glass of Pinot. I ordered a scotch.
'So, James'.

'Yes Belle?'

'Why are we here?'

'Let's just enjoy our meal first, then I will tell you everything'.

'Fine, but you had better James. Because these last fifteen years have been ... you know what, never mind'.

'No, tell me Belle, I want to know'.

'Doesn't matter anymore. It's all in the past now anyway'.
Before I can say anything, the hostess taps my shoulder.
'Your table is ready sir'. Did she just bat her eyes at me?

'Does that happen to you everywhere you go?' Belle asks as I guide her towards out table.

'Does what happen everywhere I go?' I knew exactly what she was asking, but again the sadist in me wanted to know if she was jealous.

She gives me sideways glance. 'You know very well what I mean'.

'Why Belle, are you jealous?'

'Uh, no I am not jealous. God, you have the ego as big as a house. You have nothing that I would possibly be jealous of James'.

I hold the chair for her to sit down, then take my seat opposite her.

'It's not about me, it is more about what I can give to women'.

A puzzled look crosses her face.

'Pleasure Belle. That is what I give to women. You should try it sometime, I guarantee you'll enjoy it'.

She takes a large gulp of her wine that she brought over from the bar.

'James, I can assure you I have all the enjoyment I could ever need'.

I raise my brow and know that the very next question I ask I am going to regret. But like I said before, I am a sadist.

'When was the last time you had sex?'

Probably shouldn't have asked her that question when she was taking another gulp of her wine. I grabbed the napkin off the table and wiped my face clear of the sputtered wine and spit that had projectile on me.

'Oh my god, James, I am so sorry'. She stood up to help but I told her to sit back down.

'I'm fine, really'. Throwing the now damp napkin on the table, I pick up my own drink and take a long drink from it. The waiter finally came and took our food and drink order, I was glad for the reprieve, because what I wanted to discuss with Belle tonight could go two ways.
The one way I wanted it to go, would be for her to accept and go along with my plan.
Or two, she could not only spit her drink at me again, but throw her meal all over me too.
The former I preferred. So, I decided to wait until we had finished out meal before I discussed anything with her.
We kept to small talk throughout the meal thank goodness and once I had paid the bill, we headed back outside to my car.
'James?'

'Yes?' I looked over at her, as she fastened her seatbelt.

'You've been saying you had to talk to me about something and yet I am still waiting. Can you please just get it over with right now, so I can go home and go to bed. I'm tired James and I have an early start tomorrow'.
I scratch my chin and think, because I really don't want to talk about the subject matter while I am driving. Her insistence though is grinding me down, and I know I can't keep putting it off any longer.
I unbuckle my seatbelt and turn to face her.
'Ok, I need you to listen to everything I have to say before you answer or giving me any judgement. What I am about to tell you and ask of you, will probably blow your mind and

you'll also probably think I am crazy. But this is serious, and I need your help'.

She swallowed nervously, her eyes darting back and forth. 'Ok James, I'm listening'.

'I want you to marry me'.

Her eyes widened as she licked her lips. Her eyes narrowing, then her hand lifted and slapped me across the face.

'How dare you' She bit out. Her hand went to unlock the seat belt, but I stopped her, grabbing her wrists. She struggled to get free, but no way was I letting her go.

'You said you would listen to everything I had to say, before making a judgement or answering me. So, why don't you sit still and let me finish what I started huh?'

'Fine'.

'Right, so, as I was saying. I would like you to marry me, but for appearances only. You see, my board of directors are old school and don't accept my life style anymore. Now, I am not saying that I have fucked around with every woman I have contact with Belle. I have taken many women out for dinner and the likes and I have also had sexual relationships with some too, but never anything serious. But the board is not happy with me, which is why they have given me a month to settle down'.

She stared at me, like she couldn't believe what she was hearing. So, I continued.

'If I don't settle down, then the board will kick me out of the company and I will lose everything I have built. So, you see my dilemma Belle'.

She nodded. Still a little stunned by my confession.
'So, Bella, do you think you can help me with my dilemma?'

'Can they really do that James? I mean, take your company away from you?'

'I'm afraid so. I had to garner investors to help build the company financially. They have fifty one percent of ownership between them. They all voted against me unless I clean my act up'. I scrubbed a hand down my face.
'Why me James? I am sure you have many women who could be a more ideal candidate for your needs. I mean, I haven't seen you in almost fifteen and now you're asking me to help you with this mess that your in. Is this why have come back after all this time? Because if it is, it's pretty fucked up James'.

'Look, I know you think the worst of me right now, but no, I didn't come back because of this mess I am in. I came back for you Belle, and I know I have a lot of making up to do, but I promise you, I will work hard at proving to you, that I am not leaving again. I am here to stay this time, for good'.

'But you said you wanted me to pretend. How is that going to work?'
Shit! It wouldn't work would it, because I was in love with her. Only she didn't know that. All I can do is hope that she will go along with my plan and make her fall in love with me too.
'Belle, even after all this time, I still consider you my best

friend. I couldn't ... no ... I wouldn't do this with anyone else but you. So, what do you say Belle, will you help me, please?'

'I say that I need time to think about it James. You can't expect to just turn up after all this time and ask me to marry you. And that I will just say yes to that'.

'I don't have the luxury of time, I am afraid. If you can't do this, then I lose it all. You have to give me your answer now'.
I could see the cogs going around in her head, as she peered at me.
'You know how crazy all this sounds, right? I mean, how soon are we talking for the wedding?'

'I can have a special licence by next Thursday and marry on Friday. Look I know this sounds extreme, but my livelihood is at stake here. And you're the only person I want to do this with'.

'How long?'

'Huh?'

'How long will we have to be married for, before we can get a divorce'.
I cringe, the mere thought of divorcing her made my blood turn cold. But I would have to suck it up and agree to a divorce, just so she would agree to go through with the marriage now.
'I figured one year. It's not too long, but long enough for them to think that we gave it a good go before divorcing. So, are you in, will you help me?'
Please say yes ... please say yes ... I can't believe I was

begging ... ok, so it was in my head ... but still, I never ever begged a woman for anything.

'Does Ricky know what you are planning?'

Jesus, enough with the twenty questions already!

'Yes, I spoke to him this morning about it'.

'I see. So, is that what you were talking about at my place?'

'Yes, it is. Look Belle, if you ...'

'Is that all?'

'What?'

'Was that all you talked about? You know, this morning at my place'.

Now she had me flummoxed. I knew she was getting at something but could I hell figure out what it is.

'Yes'.

'LIAR! THE PAIR OF YOU ARE FUCKING LIARS'. She whipped her belt off and before I could grab her, she was out of the car and storming down the road.

WTF!

'BELLE, WAIT! FOR GODS SAKE WOMAN WILL YOU SLOW DOWN AND TELL ME WHAT THE HELL YOU ARE ON ABOUT'.

I reached just in time to stop her running in to traffic. I wrap my arms around her waist and pull her back in to chest.

'Belle, sweetheart, stop. Please stop'. I spin her round, holding on to her hips and see tears streaming down her cheeks. I wipe them away with my thumb.

'Tell me Belle, why are you crying? I don't understand sweetheart. What's wrong? What have I done wrong or

Richard for that matter? What do you think we have lied about?'

Her sobbing was doing me in. My chest was tight with pain for the hurt in her eyes.

'Baby, please tell me, so I can make it better'. I rest my forehead on hers and close my eyes. Our lips a whisper away from each other. I dig my fingers in to her hips, pulling her closer to me.

I open my eyes and see her looking in to mine, almost pleading, begging. She licks her lips as my gaze drops to her mouth, and before I know it, our lips crash together with urgency. Our hands groping each other, like we couldn't get enough. Panting with need, if we hadn't been in the middle of the street, I would be fucking her right now up against the wall of one of these buildings.

Fuck! I had to gain control of myself right now.

I dragged my lips away from hers. Already missing the sweet taste of her plump lips.

'We need to stop. We can't do anything out here'. I gasped out. 'Come home with me Belle. I need to feel your skin next to mine'. I peppered kisses all over her face, then to the corner of her mouth. I looked in her eyes, almost pleading with her to say yes to my request.

I saw the moment when her face changed to utter shock at what had just happened, and she pulled from out of my grasp.

'I can't James. I need to go home, right now'. She turned away from me and flagged down a passing taxi and jumped in without glancing back in my direction. Leaving me stood there on the pavement, feeling like my whole world had just collapsed in on itself.

THE SEXY FAKER

ANNABELLE

Oh god, what was I thinking letting him kiss me like that! I just about made it back to my apartment, considering my thighs were clamped together and I was probably walking like I had shit myself, due to my throbbing lady bits, thanks to that hunk of meat man with his big thick pork sword pressing against my pubic bone. That started another pool party down there. Luckily for me, none of my neighbours made an appearance and I made it back free and clear of any further embarrassment.
After showering, I finally climbed into bed, feeling somewhat sorry for myself.
Why had I kissed him back so passionately? Yeah, ok, I already knew why. It was because I still wanted him, and I was kicking myself because of it. I did not want to want him, only my stupid heart wasn't listening.
I groaned and rolled over, checking my phone. I had two missed calls, a voice message and a text from James.
Did he feel embarrassed too? Was he trying to apologize for kissing and groping me? Oh god, I bet he felt guilty, didn't he? I bet he was regretting kissing me already. Crap!
I really didn't want to deal with his apologies or excuses for

what he did. So, I didn't even bother to listen to his voicemail or read the text message for that matter. I switched my phone off and tried to sleep.

Yeah, sleep not happening. After about an hour and a half of tossing and turning, I sit up abruptly, throwing my blanket off and going to the kitchen to make some hot chocolate.

As I'm waiting for the kettle to boil, there's a knock at my door. I check the time on the clock on the kitchen wall. It is almost midnight.

My stomach lurched, and I gulped, because it could only be one person at this time of night.

I hurry to my pantry door and grabbed the wooden baton from inside.

Standing against the wall next to my front door I rattle the door handle as if I am about to open. That's when a loud thud hits the door, then a moan.

'YOU BITCH! OPEN THIS FUCKING DOOR NOW OR SO HELP ME I WILL ..'. He bangs on the door again.

'I SWEAR TO GOD ANNABELLE, IF YOU DON'T OPEN THIS DOOR RIGHT NOW I WILL BREAK THE FUCKER DOWN'.

I can hear the neighbour's doors opening and muffled shouting of calls to the police in the corridor.

Another bang on my door, then it all goes quiet. I edge to the peephole in my door and peer through it. I can see the back of my ex, retreating down the corridor and towards the elevator. I let out a loud sigh of relief.

I realised a long time ago that calling the police on him didn't work. The fact that he hadn't actually done anything to me was what stopped them from being able to do anything about him. So, I had to keep a record of everything he did do, then I would eventually be able to get a restraining order. But until then, I had to put up with his once weekly drunken midnight visits.

Only Ricky knew about my ex Matt and everything he had done to me.

Then it hit me. Shit! He had been in contact with James all this time! He must have been telling him about me and what has been going on in my life all these years. For the love of god! I am going to kill him. I swear to god or lucifer, that I am going to kill Ricky, very, very slowly. Because Matt was totally off limits for discussion with anyone but me. I needed to know.

I rushed in to my bedroom and grabbed my phone off the nightstand and switched it back on. There were more missed calls from James and another two texts. I ignored them and scrolled through my contacts until I got to Ricky's name and pressed call.

He answered after five rings.

'Annabelle? What's wrong? Are you hurt or something?' I heard the panic in his voice. Of course! Slapping my forehead with the palm of my hand. He's at work and I only ever ring him at work, if there is an emergency. I also now had to admit that I know he had been in touch with his brother for all of these years.

Way to go Annabelle! Now, bite the bullet and find out what you need to know.

'Have you told James about Matt? And don't even think about lying to me, because I overheard you at my place, so I

know you have been in contact with him. What I don't get Ricky, is why you lied to me. Why you would not tell me you two were still talking?' I rushed out in one breath.
'Oh crap! ... look, I didn't lie to you about anything, I just never told you. I wanted to tell you from the start though, but James said it was best not to hurt you anymore than you already were, because he couldn't come back for a while, and he didn't know how long that would be'.

'Omission is still lying Ricky! Have you been telling him about me?'
It sounded like he had moved the phone away from his mouth, but I still heard him groaning.
'He just wanted to know that you were ok, that's it'.

'Have you told him about Matt, because James is the last person I want to know about my ex'.

'No, I have not. How could you think I would betray your confidence like that, I thought you knew me better than that'? He snapped.
I shook my head. 'I thought so too. I thought you were my best friend. But knowing now that you kept the biggest secret ever from me, I can't believe you did that to me Ricky. I don't think I can trust you, not anymore, and I don't think I can see you either. So, don't call me, don't text and definitely don't come to my place again, ok?'

'Annabe ...'
I clicked end call before he could say another word. I dropped to my knees and cried like I was grieving, because that is

exactly how it felt right now. I had grieved for the loss of my friend fifteen years ago and I am grieving again at the loss of another one. I was all alone in the world now, and even though James was back, for good he says, I still didn't trust in anything he says, just like his brother.

JAMES

Turning my head to check the time on the clock, it read seven thirty AM. I have been laying here on my bed for the last two and half hours, staring up at my ceiling. It had been four days now and Belle still wouldn't answer my calls or reply to my texts. She was apparently in hiding, because Richard hadn't seen or heard from her either. Which wasn't surprising considering that he told me what she had told him about hearing our conversation at her apartment. Thankfully she hadn't heard everything that we had discussed that morning about my plan to marry her, which was looking further and further away from ever happening.
The board would be here next week for the party for the opening of the new offices and they would be expecting my fiancée to be by my side.
 My last and only option now was to go to her apartment, and hope she opens the door. I had to make things right with her and pray that she would help me after all.
I climb off the bed and make my way in to the bathroom, turning on the shower. The hot water soothing my tired and aching muscles. I hadn't slept much the last few days, because every time I closed my eyes, I dreamed of her. Then

the guilt would wake me up in a cold sweat. There was no escaping her really. Even my days were filled with images of Belle. I felt lost at the moment, just thinking that I had lost her before I had even managed to get her, made my heart hurt. Yes, I was a complete and utter fool, and I couldn't bear it any longer.

Once I had dried off, I dressed in khaki trousers and a black T. shirt. I picked up my keys, phone and wallet and headed out to my car. I was determined to get her to at least listen to what I had to say, even though she would probably not answer the door in the first place. If it meant that I had to have a one-sided conversation through a damn closed door, then I would.

I knocked on her door and waited patiently, something I very rarely was. I knocked again then placed my ear to the door to see if I could hear any movement inside. I sighed, because I heard nothing. I checked my watch for the time as one of the neighbours peered out of her door, wearing what I would describe as a negligee. A see through one at that and nothing else under it. Essentially, she was naked.

'She's probably at work by now mister'. The woman said, winking at me.

'Right, thanks. I didn't realise it was so late in the morning'.

'That's alright sweetie. I can keep you company if you like. You know, until she comes home'. She winks at me again. I think I visibly shivered at the thought.

I made a fast getaway, waving as I passed the woman's door. Next stop, Belle's office.

I couldn't see her car parked anywhere in the car park when I arrived at the solicitors where she worked. Maybe she took a taxi or the bus, I hoped.
That smarmy bastard who I punched the last time I was here, was leaning over a desk, no doubt making a nuisance of himself again. The woman sat back, trying to get as far away as she could from him.
I strode up behind him before he had chance to see me.
'Do I need to punch you again?' The woman's eyes went wide as I quirked a brow at him when he spun round so fast, he almost fell over.
'What the hell are you doing here?' He spat out at me.

'I'm here for Belle. Is she in her office?' I looked from him to the woman still sat behind her desk.
He sneered at me, while she looked at me with sympathy. What the hell is that all about?
'You're too late'. The bastard smirked at me. He also knows something that I don't, and he better fucking tell me before I punch him again.
'Too late for what? As she left for home already?' My eyes scanned around because it was still morning. She can't have left already, unless she just bobbed in to work to pick something up.
I was about to speak again when a door behind me opened, all three of us looked round. A stoutly man with thinning hair and dark rimmed glasses, came out and stopped dead when he saw us.
'Kent, shouldn't you be working on the Danburry case?' The

THE SEXY FAKER

man narrowed his eyes. I watched the bastard squirm under the scrutinization, which made me feel fanfuckingtastic that the rest of the guys here didn't like the smarmy bastard either, by the looks of it.
'Yes sir, I was just on my way'. He scuttled away like the dirty rat he is.
The stoutly man then turned his attention back to me.
'I don't believe we have met. I'm Jonathan Bilton and you are?' He held out his hand as he approached me. So, I accepted it and shook it.
'James Jarvis. Good to meet you. I'm actually here for Belle, is she around?'

'Oh dear, I see. Well, young man you had better follow me to my office. It's too public to talk here, and what I have to say has to be done in private away from listening ears'.
WTF!
Was I going to follow him? Hell yes, because I wanted ... no, I needed to know what the hell was going on and to find out where Belle was.
I followed Jonathan in to his office. It was your typical lawyer office I guess. A large mahogany desk dominated the room. The walls were covered with built in bookcases, all dark wood and weathered looking, that was stacked with law books and old case files. A vast of windows behind where the desk was situated, overlooked a well-manicured and maintained garden. Full of flowers and plants bursting with colour.
He took a seat behind his desk. 'Come in boy and close the door. Take a seat'.

THE SEXY FAKER

I did as I was told, intrigued by this gentleman who although I had only just met, I kind of liked him.
'So, you were going to tell me where Belle was. I am all ears'.
I crossed my legs and sat back in the chair to show I was comfortable. I learned that trick years ago when I was nervous or anxious.
'How long have you know Annabelle, James?' He peered over his glasses at me.
'Most of my life. Look, whatever it is you want to tell me, just do it'. I was starting to lose some of my patience.
But Jonathan had other ideas.
'So, you know her better than anyone, is that correct?'

'I would assume so, yes. What is this about? As something happened to her?' Now the anxiety began to build within me. I could feel it slowly crawling up my body.
'No, no, nothing like that. As far as I am aware, she is fine. But there was a small incident yesterday morning when she arrived in to work'.
'What sort of incident?' All I could think of was that pervert had tried something again.

'Do you believe in honesty James?'

'Yes, I do'.

'Do you believe that Annabelle would ever lie about anything, especially something that is important and that could damage her character and reputation?'

'What? No, absolutely not!'

THE SEXY FAKER

'I didn't think so either. But it seems she has been stealing clients from under one our partners noses. I am afraid I had to dismiss her contract with us and ask her to leave our practice, effective immediately'.

I couldn't believe what I was hearing. None of this sounded like anything that Belle would do. My sneaking suspicion was that it had a lot to do with that pervert Kent Draxton and I was damned if I was going to let Belle take the blame for something she hadn't done, because of that scumbags lies.

I scrape a hand down my face and look Jonathan straight in the eye, because I never cower to anyone.

'I don't believe for a second she would have done anything like that. I do however suggest that you look in to Kent Draxton and his actions and work ethics a little more closely. Now, if you'll excuse me. I have to find Belle and make sure she is ok'.

Outside the solicitor's office I pulled out my phone and called Richard.

'Hey bro, what's up? Any news on Annabelle?'

'Yeah, you could say that. She was fired from work for stealing clients from one of the partners. I don't believe it for a second, but I can't find her anywhere. I was wondering if you had heard from her at all today or if you might know where she could be?'

'FUCK! She wouldn't steal anything from anyone, she's the most honest woman I have ever known ... wait, did you say one of the partners ...'.

THE SEXY FAKER

'Yeah'.

'That fucking dirty two-faced bastard! I bet it was that pervert Kent Draxton. He's always had it in for her since she turned him down not long after she started there. He's been hitting on her ever since. I'll fucking kill him!'

'I kind of worked that out myself, that it might be him, but you'll have to get in the queue to kill him, because I get first dibs. So, any ideas where she could be?'

The line went quiet, I couldn't even hear him breathing, so I checked to see if he had hung up.

'Richard?'

'Yeah, sorry I was just thinking, and the only place I can think of where I know she would not want to be found, is that little park where that pond is with the ducks. You know the place we used to go to when we were kids. It's the place she goes to when shit hits the fan and she needs to think … do you want me come with you?'

'No, I need to do this by myself. I'll let you know if I find her there'.

'Ok bro'.

I knew it might have been a long shot, but I had to go and see if she was there, at the park where we used to go as kids. Try and make her hear me out and hopefully I could make her feel better too and help her get her job back.

I jump in my car, my blood boiling, rage emanating throughout my body to the point where I am shaking. I am in two minds to go back in there and do the job of pummelling

THE SEXY FAKER

my fists in to that scumbag. My knuckles are white as I clench the steering wheel, and as I start driving towards the destination, I begin to think back to the last time we were there at the park we used to go to years ago.

It was the hottest summer we had had for some years, what with British weather being unpredictable, we would make the most of it and head down to the park with the duck pond. I was sixteen and Richard and Belle were fourteen. Mum had kicked us out of the house from under her feet, as she called it. So, we grabbed the picnic blanket from the pantry, some snacks and drinks and headed out to our secret place, that only us three knew about.

There were never many if any, people about at the park with the duck pond, because it was so small, no-one really bothered about it. So, we had claimed it as our own.
We had changed in to our swimsuits and shorts, so we could lay out on the blanket and sunbathe. Mum had thrown a bottle of sun block at me and told us to make sure we covered ourselves in it, so as not to get burned.

'Hey, Belle, throw me another bag of space invaders'

'James, you have had two already, don't be so greedy and your mum will go mad at you if you don't eat your tea later. So, no, I will not throw you another bag, anyway there's only three left and the one is Ricky's, the others are mine'. She pulled her tongue out at me and ran off towards the pond with the bags in her hand.

'RICHARD, GET HER!'

We both chased after her, running as fast as we could because she had a lead on us. She kept looking behind her and laughing, then stopped at the edge of the pond, holding the bags of space invaders over the water.

'NO, DON'T DO IT BELLE, YOU LITTLE SHIT!' I screamed at her.

'Mum will ground you for swearing at Annabelle'. My little brother informed me.

'I don't care. We need to get those crisps off her before she dumps them in the pond. Come on, you go to the left and I'll go to the right. We can block her in and grab the bags'.

Belle was giggling when we approached at either side of her. Her feet were teetering on the pond edge as we neared. Richard nodded at me to let me know he would creep up behind her when she looked at me.
He rushed up towards her at the same time as she whipped her head around to him, it was then that I began to run towards her too. Just as we both reached at the same time, she squealed and lost her balance and began to fall in to the water.

'SHIT! GRAB HER RICHARD, QUICK!'

We both went to grab her, her hands flayed out and caught us on our shorts waistband, dragging us with her in to the pond.
We managed, with moderate decorum, to get out of the water and laid out on the grassy bank. Out of breath and laughing our heads off.
Richard was to my left and I turned to Belle on my right as

she turned her head towards me with the biggest smile on her face. It was then, when I looked at her happy face, with water dripping down her face, her long blonde hair clinging to her head and cheeks that things changed. I didn't see her as my best friend with a sense for fun and great sense of humour, I saw a beautiful girl with a beautiful smile and beautiful heart.

I turned in to the carpark. The park had obviously expanded since the last time I was here. Besides the carpark, there was picnic tables and all the shrubbery that had kept our place a secret for so long, was no all trimmed back. Beds of flowers and brightly coloured plants and shrubbery, lined a pathway to the pond. Which now had seating and benches around it. The ducks were still there thank goodness, although I doubt they were the same ducks from when we were kids.
There was a few people mulling around, enjoying the day as I made my way along the path.
I rounded the bend that was a blind spot of tall trees. It was then that I saw the long flowing blonde hair of a woman, sat on one of the benches with her back to me. A woman I would know anywhere ... Belle.
I slowly made my way to her, not wanting to just charge over to her and startle her in to running.
When I got nearer, she must had heard my approach and turned her head to face me. Her eyes widened in shock at first, but then she let out a deep sigh, her shoulders sagging in defeat.

'Hi Belle'.

'How did you find me James?'

'I went to your work'. That was all I needed to say, considering the understanding look on her face.

'I guess you remembered then'.

'Yeah. You used to always come here when you needed to think or just de-stress. I figured this would be where you were after my conversation with Jonathan Bilton'.

'I don't know what to do James. I lost my job and my best friends, I may as well lose my apartment and have done with it'.

'What the hell are you talking about? Richard and I will always be here for you, no matter what. Don't you get it? We aren't going anywhere, so you haven't lost us, ok? As for your job, well we both know that little weasel Draxton had something to do with that. But don't worry, that snake will get what's coming to him, mark my words'.

'James, why did you and Ricky lie to me? I mean, you were both remiss in telling me that you were still in contact. I guess I don't understand why you both kept me out of the loop. I know he told you about me, about how I was doing over the years. It doesn't seem fair that I knew nothing about you'.

'Look, Belle. Some shit was going on back then, stuff that has taken me years to sort out, and eventually I will tell you all about it, just now isn't the right time'.

THE SEXY FAKER

She studied my face. The cogs working over time in her brain. I knew she had a million and one questions she wanted to ask. But I also knew her respect for my feelings would stop her right now, until I was ready.

'Ok James' She blew out a long breath and stared out across the pond. 'What now?'

'Are we ok Belle? You, me and Richard I mean, are you ok with us?'

'I guess so. I just wish ... well, you know what I wish. But I'm good ... we're good, don't worry'.

I patted her knee and sat back next to her on the bench, watching the ducks and the world go by for the next half an hour.
She was the first to speak again.

'James'.

'Yes?'

'Do you still need my help? You know, the whole fake married thingy?'

'Yeah, I do actually. And it can just be a fake engagement actually'. I laughed, because saying it out loud made it as absurd as it was.

'I'll do it. I mean, if you still want me to do it, that is. Unless you have got someone else, I mean ...'.

I cut her off. 'No, there is no-one else I would rather be fake engaged to than you'.

We both laughed then. God, I missed her laugh so much. I missed her full stop.

'I have an idea, why don't we go to dinner and discuss everything. The board will be here in a few days, so we need to prepare'.

'Sounds like a plan'.

'How about I pick you up at your place around eight. We can go to that new place that just opened on Grant road'.

'Oh, you mean Betsy bistro? Yeah, I would love to go there. Tina from work ... I mean, where I used to work, she went there last week and said the fish dishes are to die for'.
How could I deny her, with the excitement in her voice, she was practically bouncing with joy.
I was just glad to see that smile on her face again. And I intended to keep it there, hopefully for the rest of our lives.

JAMES

I picked Belle up at eight as promised. The dress she was wearing was something else. A blue bodycon that matched her eyes. Her hair was loose and had been slightly curled at the ends. She hardly had any make-up on from what I could tell, but her lips had been covered in a deep red colour and very kissable. I was instantly hard when she opened the door, I couldn't take my eyes off her. she had cracked a joke about how her eyes were up here, as she pointed at them with her finger, because my eyes had scanned her delectable body with admiration.

We arrived at Betsy Bistro twenty minutes late and seated at our table immediately.

The atmosphere was quiet and chilled as other dinner guests spoke quietly, making the place feel relaxed, and you feel comfortable in the surroundings.

'Wow, this place is lovely James. Thank you for bringing me'.

'It's my pleasure. Shall we check out the menu and order, or would you like something to drink first?'

'We can order our food and drink at the same time. Then you can tell me everything I need to know about the board

members and the plan for this fake engagement'.
The waiter came to our table for our order. We both ordered the monkfish with asparagus, jersey royals with mint en papilotte.

'So, tell me everything'. She urged, when the waiter finally left after filling our glasses with a pinot.

'Ok, so I told you the gist of what I needed before. The thing is, I have never had a serious relationship. I have had relations with women ... you know what, you don't need to know that part. Anyway, the board thinks my lifestyle has been discrediting the company and we could lose contracts if I don't shape up and settle down. They are talking about kicking me out if I don't, so essentially I can lose everything I have built'. I scratch my chin, then rub the back of my neck, because I know what I am about to tell her, I also know she isn't going to like it.

'Ok, so you need me to pretend to be your fiancée, right?'

'Yeah, here's the thing. I kind of already told them you were, and they expect a wedding in the next couple months. Sorry'. I smiled sheepishly at her, as she shook her head.

'James, are you saying that we have to actually get married? This is not just an engagement?'

'Yeah, sorry. Maybe I should have mentioned that sooner. Look, we don't have to go the hole hog, so to speak. Just a quiet ceremony. The board and their wives will be there too of course, I guess to make sure it really is happening ... me settling down I mean. I also want you to know that I will draw up some kind of contract for us to sign in regard to helping me out and I will compensate you, so don't worry about that. It will only have to last for a few months too, then we can get the marriage annulled or divorce, whatever. And I also promise to stay faithful to you while we are married, and I expect the same from you. All this will be stated in the contract'.

I saw her gulp, then reach for her glass of wine, taking a large gulp and swallowing.

'I have one question James'.

'What is that Belle?'

'Are you expecting us to have sex, while we are married?' I could see the fear in her eyes. Jesus! Was she really that scared of me? Or was she scared of her feelings for me maybe? Either way, I had to make her believe she had nothing to be scared of from me. I would share how I felt about her, but not before she was willing to share how she felt about me.

I saw how she as looked at me since we were teenagers and seeing her again after all these years, that look is still there when she sees me.

'No Belle, I don't expect us to have sex with each other. Not unless you want to that is, I mean, I am willing if you are'. Maybe I shouldn't have said that last bit when she was taking a drink, because now I was plastered. AGAIN! With a mixture of her spit and wine. Will I never learn!

'Fuck, James. Why do you do that every time?'

THE SEXY FAKER

'Must be glutton for punishment I guess. Anyway, do we have a deal Belle, because I am seriously hanging on by the skin of my teeth here'.

She wiped her chin with the napkin and placed it on the table.

'Yes, we have a deal James'.

I breathed out a sigh of relief and took her hand in mine, lifting it to my lips and kissing her soft skin on the back of her hand.

'Thank you, Belle. You have literally saved my life'.

I had planned on seducing her tonight when I took her home, but after the sex conversation, I am pretty sure she wouldn't be up for it. Looks like my work is cut out for me. I had to tread carefully so she wouldn't back out.
So when I dropped her off, I headed back to my place and took a very long cold shower, which didn't even work, because I was now laid in bed with a raging hard on again, after taking care of the one I had had all night in the shower. All I had to do was picture her face and I was hard. So, I closed my eyes and pulled down my pyjama shorts and took myself in hand. Stroking gently and slowly at first.
I pictured Belle straddling me, her hair falling forward as she grinded against my erection. I could feel the heat from her pussy as her juices coated my cock. Her tits bounced as she rode me. Lifting one hand, I pinched her nipple while my other hand held her hip tight, my fingers digging in to her flesh.

THE SEXY FAKER

I could feel her inner walls clench me. Her moans becoming louder along with my own, as her orgasm spiralled out of control. Both my hands are on her hips now as I lifted my own hips to meet hers as I fucked her hard.

Suddenly I felt my balls tighten, my grip on my cock becoming more demanding as I stroke faster for my release. I come like a volcano erupting, strands shooting across my abdomen. Panting until my heart rate diminishes to a normal beat again, and my breathing becomes regular.

Fuck! She was the only woman who could have this effect on me. All I knew was that at some point within this mockery of an engagement and marriage, I would finally have Belle in every way possible. I wanted her body, heart and soul. I loved the bones of her, and I would make her see that I am hers, and she is mine.

THE SEXY FAKER

ANNABELLE

What was I thinking agreeing to this plan of his! I didn't sleep a wink last night. After James dropped me off, all I could think about was what this fake marriage would be like. How was I supposed to act around him, especially if I was going to have to live with him until this debacle was over. The problem was, I didn't think I wanted it to be over, I hoped at some point that he would see how I felt about him. But he hadn't even said anything about feelings and only mentioned sex. How long I could hold off on not having sex with him, I didn't know. It was going to be difficult, I knew that much. All I knew was that if we did have sex, then it would be harder for me to not get my heart broken when the marriage ended, because my feelings for him were getting deeper & stronger by the day.

I had to try and push my feelings and any reservations to one side. He was my best friend and I had promised to help him with his plan to keep his company and the board members off his back.

I rolled out of bed, and headed to the bathroom, almost tripping over my shoes I had worn last night. I kicked them across the floor and preceded to stump my toe on the floor, bending it back. Yeah, so, now I am hopping about like a fucking kangaroo and squealing in agony. I'm just glad there is no-one here to see me.

Knock ... knock ... knock.

Oh, for fucks sake!
I hop down the hall way to my door and peer through the peephole.

Great ... James!

'JUST A MINUTE'. I called through the closed door. The last thing I needed right now was him to see me like this.
I looked down at myself and what I had slept in. Yep, typical, I would have to be wearing my hello kitty nightshirt. Why couldn't I have had on like a negligee or something like sexy lingerie. Anything but my stupid hello kitty nightshirt, for crying out loud!
So, I do the only thing I can think of, and run back to my bedroom, grab my thick robe and wrap it around me quickly before going to open the door.

'Hi James, come in'. I am trying not to stand on my right foot, because my toe is throbbing like a Tom and Jerry cartoon. Only I look more like Quasimodo at the moment, as I stand slightly twisted over.
James enters and spins around watching me as I close the door. He looks at me up and down, then back down at my feet and my bulbous red toe.

'What the hell have you done to your toe?'

THE SEXY FAKER

I groan. Because the last I want or need, is sympathy from him.

'Belle, what have you done?' He takes the two steps to stand in front of me. Then in another second, he has lifted me up in to his arms, and is carrying me to the sofa. My arms cling tightly around his neck.
He sits next to me and lifts my foot on to his knee and begins inspecting. I try to pull it away, but he holds on firm to my ankle.

'Don't move Belle, let me see'. He touches my foot and toe tenderly, then leans forward and kisses the top of my toe.

'I stumped my stupid toe on the stupid floor before I came to answer the door'.

'So, I see. But I've kissed it better now. Is there anywhere else that you ... hurt, that may need kissing better?'
I pull my foot from out of his grasp and took my legs underneath me.

'Why are you here James?'
He stares at me a long moment. He bites the corner of his bottom lip. God, I want to bite that lip myself, then suck on it and maybe his tongue too. Yeah, his tongue. I'd like to suck on his cock too, I bet he tastes divine ….

'Belle, did you hear what I said?'
I blink and look at him. A smirk on his face, when I realise I must have spaced out. And is that drool coming out of the side of my mouth.
Shit! I quickly wipe it away with the back of my hand.

'Belle, were you drooling over me?' His light chuckle did nothing but ignite my already embarrassment.

'Huh? What? No, of course not. Don't flatter yourself James. What do you want anyway?'
He scraped his fingers through his hair, looking down, then back at me. Taking an envelope out from his inside pocket and dropping it on to my lap.

'I thought I would bring you the contract to look over before you signed it. Hopefully we can get that done by tonight, so we can organise the wedding in the next few weeks. Is that ok?'
I let out a deep sigh. This was really happening. I just hoped my heart wouldn't get crushed in the process.

'Sure, the sooner the better right?'

'Right. The other thing I wanted to discuss with you is the intimacy'.

'What do you mean?' I narrowed my eyes at him.

'Well, just that to make this look real, we have to touch and kiss and hug, stuff like that. You know, in public I mean, for the board to believe we are for real'.

'Right, yes. I guess that makes sense. Ok, we can do that'. I couldn't help but look down at his crotch then. Something I wish I hadn't done, because it was clear to see, that he had a hard on, and it looked about to pop his zipper.
His brow lifted. His eyes looking at my lips as I licked them. I was totally lost in the moment, and if he had spoken right

then, the bubble would have burst, and I didn't want it to.
I couldn't help myself. Leaning forward, I reached for his zipper and slowly pulled it down, then unfastened his button. His breath hitched, as I stroked a finger up and down his length over his boxers.
Before I could think, I pulled the waistband down and gripped him, slowly my hand moved up and down his cock. I looked up at him, his head fell back, and his eyes were closed. His chest, rising and falling quicker with every stroke of my hand.
I could feel myself getting wet, knowing it was me that was having this effect on him. Making him hard and turned on.
I needed a taste. So, I leaned over and swiped the head of his cock with my tongue. He was slightly salty and musky and the smell and taste of him made me even wetter.

'Fuck! Belle, that feels good'. He moaned with pleasure, as I dipped my head again, only this time I took him in to my mouth. He grew harder, if that is possible.
I wrap my fingers around the thick base of his length, as my I drag my mouth up and suck on the head. I take him deep again and relish the sound of his pleasurable moans.
He watches me now, as I lick and suck, devouring every inch of him.
I tease him now, taking him to the hilt, the head hitting the back of my throat. Then I wrap my lips just around the tip while I pump him for a few strokes, then take all of him in to my mouth again.
I can tell by the way he juts his hips up and the noises he is

making, that he is close. So, my hand works him with a firm grip, as I lightly hold the mushroom head in my warm wet lips.

I keep a steady rhythm now, until I can not only see and hear the build up to his orgasm, but I can feel it too.

'Belle, you need to stop. I'm going to come'.

I look at him and smile, keeping the pace. He grabs my hair in his fists, and just like that, he breaks free on to my tongue and down my throat.

When his breathing had levelled out, he pulls me up on to his lap and kisses me. Our tongues entwined and knowing he can probably taste himself just turns me on even more.

I'm straddling him, my nightshirt risen to my thighs, showing my bare skin to him.

His hands travel down my front, untying the belt to my robe, then pushing it off my shoulders. He breaks the kiss and his lips travel down my neck.

I hear a soft chuckle and look down at him.

CRAP!

'Well, I can honestly say I have never been turned on before by hello kitty'.

'Dammit! I wasn't expecting company this morning, James. Stop laughing at my night attire and kiss me, now'.

His hands lift to my cheeks and he pulls my face to his, kissing me gently.

'Are you sure you want to do this Belle. Because once I start, I don't think I'll be able to stop'. His eyes penetrated mine. I knew then that I wouldn't want him to stop, if my life depended on it. Right now, all I wanted was to feel James inside of me. Nothing else mattered at this moment.

'Yes James. I want you inside me right now'.

He shoves his hand in to my hair, cradling the back of my head. His mouth devours mine. His other hand inches up my thigh, his thumb almost touching my wet folds, making me shudder.
My robe had fallen off my arms and on to the floor. I needed to be naked, I needed him naked. To feel our skin touching. I grabbed the hem of my nightshirt and pulled it over my head, dropping it to the floor.
The only thing separating his cock from entering me, was my panties.
James eyes widened. Darkening and hooded with lust, as he stared at my breast.

'Fuck, Belle. You are beautiful. So beautiful sweetheart'.

I ached for him to touch me, so I arched my back, pushing my breast forward. He didn't disappoint me. He lowered his head and took a nipple between his lips, tugging on it. I let out a moan as he slid his fingers beneath the fabric of my panties. I practically bucked in his arms when he found my slick hot slit. His thumb found my clit and began to swirl as he drove two fingers inside me. I cried out as my inner walls clenched around his fingers like a vice.

'Oh my god, James. I'm going to come'. I panted out. I felt dizzy. My entire body tensed as the orgasm crashed through my body.

THE SEXY FAKER

No-one had ever made me feel like that before. My past boyfriends were always so, wham bam thank you ma'am! James held on to me tightly as I came down from the bliss I felt.

'That's it sweetheart. Now I am done with the starter, let's take this to the bedroom so I can make you come again and again'.

He picked me up and carried me through to my bedroom, laying me gently on the bed.
He undressed. He stood before me like a Greek god. All tanned and toned. I didn't think eight packs were possible until I saw his, but fuck did his abs look good. I leaned over and traced a finger over the bumps and licked my lips because I so wanted to run my tongue over the ridges.

'Another time'. He said, as if reading my mind. 'Right now, I need my cock inside of you'.

I wasn't going to argue. I laid back and opened my legs for him. I didn't care how slutty it looked, I wanted him.

'Beautiful. I've waited a long time for this'. He whispered. I barely heard him.

He reached down and grabbed his trousers off the floor, reaching inside a pocket, he pulled out a condom. Then climbed on to the bed, kneeling between my legs and looked down at me. Ripping the packet, he took out the condom and rolled it on, before crawling over my body and lining himself up with my entrance.

THE SEXY FAKER

He wasn't the only one had been waiting a long time for this.
Wait! Did he say he had been waiting a long time for this?
Could this mean he had wanted me the same as I had wanted him, back when we were teenagers?
Could it be possible he felt the same way as I did?
Or was I just wishful thinking?

'Belle, are you ok?'

'Huh? Oh, yeah sorry. Carry on'.

The amused look on his face said it all. I must have spaced out again. But before I had chance to say or do anything else, he pushed in to me, in one long hard thrust.

'Fuck, Belle. So wet, so tight ... ahh'.

He stayed still. But I needed him to move, I didn't care that I hadn't fully adjusted to his size.

'Please, James, fuck me'.

He didn't take no more persuading.

'I don't think I could go slow if I wanted to. You feel too damn good'.

Lifting my legs up, he placed my feet on his shoulders, making it so he could push in even deeper. The new angle had him hitting the right spot, as he drew out and then slammed back in to me. It had me arching my back and gripping on to his biceps hard, digging my nails in to his flesh. We fucked that hard, I worried my bed would break under the punishment.

THE SEXY FAKER

He moved his hand between us and pressed on to my clit with just the right amount of pressure, it sent me almost flying off the bed.

'Oh god, oh god, oh god'. I couldn't help chanting.

'Not fucking god sweetheart. Say my name when you come, and only my name'.
He pounded me harder. Faster. My legs went tense as I came, my pussy clenching his cock as he swelled inside me and arched his back. His head thrown back, he cried out my name, he pulsed inside me as his orgasm ripped through him also.
His head dipped into my neck. Sweat beading down his back as I ran my fingers lightly up and down it, damping the tips of my fingers.
Once our breathing had become stable again, he rolled off me and laid beside me. His hand took hold of mine and entwined his fingers with mine.

'Wow. Just ... wow!' He said, turning his head to face me and placing a kiss on my kiss. 'I knew it would be good, but that was fucking amazing Belle'.

'Can we do that again?'

His grin was wide and a devilish one at that.
'You better believe it sweetheart. But first, I am going to taste you. I need to lick that delectable pussy of yours and I want you to come on my tongue'.

'Then you better get on with it Mr Jarvis, because I am not sure how much longer I can wait'.

THE SEXY FAKER

Without another word, he pounced on me and rolled us, so that I was straddling him. His hands grabbed my ass and he began to pull me up his chest.

'James, what are you doing?'

Suddenly I was hovering over his face. His fingers digging in my ass cheeks.

'I want your juicy pussy on my mouth now'.

I groaned out and positioned myself over him. The first lick of his tongue came quickly. Brushing lightly over my lips and making my body shudder.
He moved his hands from my ass and over my hips, gliding his fingers under my breasts, then over them until he reached my peaked nipples. Taking then between his fingers, he tweaked and pulled on them.
His tongue began to lap and delve within me. He fucked me with his tongue then slid it over my swollen clit. I bucked and writhed on his face. Grinding as he licked at my bud.

'Oh fuck ... James, I'm coming'.

My body did flips as I came hard. His fingers tugging my nipples hard as he continued to lap at my lips through my orgasm, making it even more tense.

'That is the best fucking, most beautiful thing I have ever seen. Belle, you blow my mind sweetheart. Now, let me make you come again'.

And he did. Many times, throughout the day. Until we were both sated.

JAMES

I looked over at a sleeping Belle. Her hair splayed across the pillow, her lips slightly parted. She was laid on her front and the sheet had slid down, baring her creamy white back. The moonlight casting shadows across it and twinkling across her skin.

I still couldn't believe I had finally been able to make love to the only woman I had ever loved, and I had every intention on doing this every day from now on. I wanted to fall asleep with her in my bed every night and wake up to her every morning. I was going to make this happen.

I needed to use the bathroom, so I got out of bed as gently as possible and when I had finished in there, I went to grab a glass of water.

Feeling a little peckish, I stuck my head in the fridge to see if there were any left overs, when I couldn't find anything, I saw there was a pantry door to the left and opened it.

The first thing that caught my eye, was what looked like an old wooden police baton, leaning against the wall just inside the door way. What the hell! Why did she have that? The apartment block she lived in was relatively a safe area and she had dead bolts and locks galore too. No-one was getting in here unless she wanted them in.

A few minutes later I had my answer.

BANG! BANG! BANG!

WTF!

Belle came rushing from the bedroom and straight to the pantry. She didn't even see me standing by the kitchen island as she swung open the door and grabbed the baton. Turning to face me, she visibly jumped.

'FUCK ... FUCKITY ...FUCK! What the hell are you doing standing there in the dark? You scared the living daylights out of me!'

'Sorry, but who the fuck is that banging on your door at ...' I checked the time on the clock on the wall behind me. '... midnight?'

'Crap, I should have told you sooner I guess, but ..'.

'ANNABELLE ... YOU BITCH ... OPEN THIS FUCKING DOOR NOW'.

Whoever this scumbag was, was in for a fucking rude awakening. I put my finger to my lips and shushed Belle.

'What are you doing?' She whispered.

'Let me get rid of the prick. Whoever he is, won't be bothering you again after tonight'.

'No, James. Don't. You don't understand. I ... I mean ... I .. he's my ex who can't let it go that I ended it because of his drinking. Matt is an alcoholic. I guess I stayed with him too long, hoping he would change, but he never did. I don't want you making things worse'.

'BITCH ... OPEN THIS DOOR NOW!'

'Go back to the bedroom Belle and let me deal with this, ok?'

She nodded, handed me the baton and walked back to the bedroom as slowly as humanly possible. She kept looking over her shoulder at me and biting that goddam bottom lip of hers. I knew she was worried. Concerned. But I had dealt with scum like him before when I was in L.A. and I was dammed if I was going to let anyone or anything for that matter get in the way of me being with Belle. Even if I am a little pissed that Richard hadn't told me about this dickhead, at least now I knew and could deal with it. And I would deal with my brother later.

I walked over to the door and laid the baton against the wall, then peered through the peep hole.

The bastard was peering right back at me, as if he could see me.

'I CAN HEAR YOU BREATHING BEHIND THE DOOR ANNABELLE. OPEN THIS FUCKING DOOR RIGHT NOW'.

He didn't look that big from what I could I see. Yeah, I think I could probably take this guy easy. He was dressed in a suit of all things. Who the fuck dresses in a suit at this time of night? It was also pretty obvious that he was drunk as a skunk too and there would be no reasoning with him. My options were limited. I had three choices as I saw it. One, I could kick the

THE SEXY FAKER

shit out of him and threaten him, if he ever came back to bother her again. Two, I could get dressed and force him to a nearby all night café and force coffee down him, so then I might get to make him see reason, or I could just call the police and get his sorry ass thrown in the clinker for the night. That would probably be the best answer, he would give him chance to think about what he was doing and see just how pathetic he was.

To be honest, I don't think I could let Belle go without a fight if we were ever in that situation. Although I know I would definitely go about it in a different way to this asshole.

Instead I went with a fourth option.

I took a deep breath, unlocked the door and opened it. I was buck naked and stood there glaring at him, with my brows raised in question.

'WHO THE FUCK ARE YOU?'

'Please keep the noise down. There are people trying to sleep'.

'WHO. THE. FUCK. ARE. YOU?'

Really, this guy was as thick as shit and it was time to put him straight and get rid.

'I'm Belle's fiancé. Who are you?'

'NO FUCKING WAY!'

'Yes, so if you don't mind, don't ever come here again. Especially shouting your mouth off and disrespecting my fiancée. Because next time I will put you down on your sorry pathetic ass. Do I make myself clear?'

'I didn't know she had found someone else. Fuck! I thought if I could just talk to her, she would give me a second chance. Fuck!'

'Look, I get it. She's one of a kind. But she has moved on and it is time you did too'.

'Shit! Yeah, I guess you're right. I seriously need to sort my life out. It's just ... Annabelle is ... was, everything to me. I just didn't know how to handle the break up. I know drinking isn't the answer ... Sorry man, I'll go. You won't see me here again, I promise'.

'Good to know'.

He scratched his head and set off back down the hall way towards the lift. Stopping and turning back to me.
'Hey. You know she never let's anyone call her Belle, not even me. I reckon she must really love you if she let's you'.
With a resigned look in his eyes, he nodded, turned and left.

Could he be correct in his assumption? That Belle loves me? Hang on a minute ... what the hell am I thinking! Why the fuck was I even considering what this jerk said to me about Belle?
Because I was in to wishful thinking, I guess. Fuck!

I heard the bedroom door open as I spun around and picked up the baton. Belle was headed my way, with a deer in headlights appearance as she looked down at the baton I was holding in my hand. She had pulled on that hello kitty nightshirt from earlier.

'Hey, how are you doing?' I met her halfway and wrapped an arm around her waist. Pulling her in to my chest.

'What did you do James?'

I could feel her shaking in my arms. But I realised it wasn't because she was cold, it was because she thought I had done something to her ex. Like, beat him with the baton.

'All I did was explain to him the situation and that he wasn't welcome here anymore. I told him it was time to move on because you have and that you have no intentions of ever getting back together with him'. Yeah, ok, what I told her, and what I actually said wasn't true, but she didn't need to know that.

'Oh, ok. What did he say?'

'He agreed with me and said he was going to finally straighten himself out. I think he realised he had no hope of getting you back'.

'Ok, well that's good. I'm glad he's finally come to his senses and getting some help'. Her shoulders visibly slumped in relief at this news.
But I was still curious about something and needed to know.

'Can I ask you something Belle, and I want you to be truly honest with your answer ok?'

'Sure. What do you want to know?'

'Him, Matt. Why did you stay with for so long? It's clear to see he's at rock bottom now. You are the strongest person I know. I guess I just don't understand why you would put yourself through all that'.

Her eyes glazed over as she became deep in thought. Trying to voice her answer, to make me understand her reasoning. I could sense her hesitation as her body stiffened in my arms. Taking a deep breath, she looked up in to my eyes and began to speak.

'Well, because I thought he could ... no, would change. He wasn't always like this, drinking I mean.
It was really great in the beginning. He was so kind and generous with his time and his emotions.
I'm not sure when the drinking started, to be honest or when it began to get worse. He was always so good at hiding it at first. Then he started to stay late at the office and come home wasted. I thought he was cheating on me, but one night when he said he had to work late again, I went to his office, and there he was, drinking whiskey straight from the bottle.
Apparently the cleaning staff have had to wake him up from his drunken slumber on many occasions and call a taxi for him to get him home.
Two years James, that is how long I stuck it out, to try and help him. I guess you can't help someone who doesn't want to be helped. I gave up on him after I had had enough of his verbal abuse'.

I blanched at her words that made my blood begin to boil. 'Did he hit you?' I said through gritted teeth. Because if I found out he had laid a single finger on her, I would hunt him down and kill the bastard.

'What? No, nothing like that'. She shakes her head.

'You must have loved him very much to put up with all that you did'.

'I don't know ... I think I loved the idea of him. I think towards the end, when I had had enough of his abuse and drinking, I just pitied him. I guess I loved him in my own way, but I wasn't in love with him ... god! That sounds bad doesn't it?'

'No. You cared for him Belle, cared enough to try and help him, even if he didn't want it. Maybe now though, this is his wake-up call and he will finally get the help he needs'.

'I hope so. He's a good man underneath all that and he deserves to get well again and be happy ... can I ask you something?'

I tightened my hold on her and gave her squeeze, placing a kiss on her forehead.

'Of course, anything'.

'Is that a baton in your hand or are you just pleased to see me?'

The little minx giggled. So, I smacked her ass and chased her back in to the bedroom.

ANNABELLE

When I woke up this morning, I was sore all over, thanks to the marathon sex I had with James all night long. Oh, and not forgetting shower sex this morning before he left to take care of some business.
If this is what being married to James was going to be like, then I was in for a real treat. I had signed the contract this morning. It stipulated that upon marriage, he was to give me £250.000. I was in shock when I read that part, so, of course, I told him I didn't want the money, that I was helping him out as a friend. But then he reminded me of my jobless situation and that the money would help me get by until I could find employment with another firm.
How could I argue with that?

I was now sat on my sofa having a cup of coffee and waiting for Ricky to drop by. He had called me earlier to say he would be coming in to see me on his way home from work and told me to get the coffee on, he was bringing blueberry muffins and pastries. God, I loved that guy, just not in the same way as James though. He just knew everything about me. My likes and dislikes for one. The fact that I crave blueberry muffins and coffee for one. He knows that I am allergic to apples, yeah, I know I am weird and I don't know of anyone else allergic to apples either. He knows I enjoy action movies over Rom-Coms and that sweet popcorn is my vice. That my favourite flowers are Daffodils and my shoe and bag collection is over the fifty mark and counting. He knows I snore lightly and talk in my sleep, due to the many times we have crashed at each other's places.

Ricky is my best friend in the whole world and a brother to me, even though we had that weird thing go on the other day in my bedroom. I think he just got confused about what his feelings for me were, because his brother was back in town. Anyway, with the air now cleared, we were back to being best friends again thank goodness.

A knock at the door brings me out of my thoughts.
I open it with a big stupid grin on my face.

'Hey Ricky. What's cracker lacking?'

'Coffee and blueberry muffins, as if you didn't know' He said, with an eye roll.

'Gimme them now'. I reached for the bag in his left hand and grabbed the coffee from his right.

'At least let me get in the door first woman, before you attack me'.

'Ha Ha, very funny' I say, then ram the muffin in to my mouth, taking a large bite.
Ricky looks on at me intently. His face blank from emotion but staring at me none the less.

'What?!'

'Nothing'. He shrugs and plonks down on my sofa, resting a arm on the backrest.

'Are you working tonight?' I asked him, before dropping on the seat next to him, tucking my feet under me and putting my coffee on the coffee table.

'Nope, so do you want to do something later? Go see a movie and something to eat?'
I grimaced, because I knew James was coming back later and he had suggested taking me out tonight, then spending the night at his place.

'Ahh. Sorry, I can't. James is taking me out'.

'Eh? When did this happen? I thought he was your mortal enemy?'

'Yeah, things have kind of … changed between us. Look, don't be mad. Please, don't be mad ok?'
He narrowed his eyes at me.

'Why would I be mad Annabelle? What's going on?'
Yeah, by the expression on his face, he was already mad, and I hadn't even told him anything yet.

'Well, you see … ermm … I … I mean we, as in your brother and I … we are … ermm …'.

'For fucks sake Annabelle. Spit it out!'
Ok, maybe now isn't the right time to tell him about what James plans were and that part of that plan was to marry me. Or … was it possible that James could have already told him

his plans? Was that why he was so angry before I had even told him anything?

Shit!

'What do you know about your brothers plans and his company?'

Ricky let out an exasperated breath and laid his head back, closing his eyes for a second. When he lifted his head back up and faced me, opening his eyes. That's when I saw it.

His hurt.

He swallowed hard. A slow disbelieving shake of his head followed as he gave me a long-pained look then turned his head away, breaking eye contact.

FUCK!

He knew. He knew every damn thing. And it was clear to see on his face.

'Ricky I ...'.

'Leave it. I get it, ok? You have been in love with James since we were kids. I know it has always been him for you, so don't worry. I get it. Just ...'. He averted his eyes again, taking a deep breath. 'Just be careful. I don't want you getting hurt and thinking that this is more than it is'.

'More than it is? What do you mean?' I turn my palms up and tilt my head to the side.

'I mean that my brother is doing all this to save his business and not because you think he loves you'.

I slump back in to the cushion. I snort dismissively and cross my legs. I am trying not to show just how much his words have affected me. But I can't stop the stabbing sensation in my chest. He may as well have pushed a knife through my heart.

I had to question though, was I deluding myself to think that James had feelings for me? More than that of a friend? I was kidding not only my head, but my heart too. I had to think of this as a business transaction. It was after all, what I had agreed to.

My mind was made up. My feelings had to be pushed back in to that box where they had been all these years and locked away forever. Because James hadn't lied to me about his plans, he had been pretty honest about he was intending. It was me that had started to bring emotions and feelings in to it, without him even knowing about it. I had to protect my heart no matter what.

'Look, Ricky. I know you mean well but, I don't love James and I know he doesn't love me. This plan of his is me just helping out a friend. We've talked about the shit that went down and I have forgiven him for that. So, I …'.

'Wait … what? You mean James has told you why he left, and you forgave him? Just like that?' His posture stiffened, and his mouth slackened.

Crap! He thinks I already know why James left all those years ago. If I play my cards right, I will be able to find out the truth from Ricky why James really left without a backward glance.

THE SEXY FAKER

'Oh, yeah. I mean it took a lot of persuading on his part, of course. But once he told me all the ins and outs and everything, well, it all made sense I guess. So, it was easy to forgive him'. His lips pressed together as he studied me carefully. I could see the wheels turning in his head as he narrowed his eyes at me. His grimace now turning in to a wide grin. Then wider still, as he leaned forward and pointed a finger at me.
'He hasn't told you, has he? Clever, very clever Annabelle, trying to get me to confess his secrets'. He stood up shaking his head.
'I'm out of here. I need to sleep. Just remember what I said, ok? I don't want you getting hurt again. He won't mean to do it, but he will do it'. With kiss to my cheek and a sad smile, he left me to ponder on what he had said about James.

My feelings for James had been getting stronger by the day. But after what Ricky had said, I knew I had to keep them in check. I knew all James needed from me was to be his pretend fiancée and then wife for a period of time, so he could keep his company. This was going to be the hard part, because we would have to live together.
Sex hadn't been part of the agreement, but hell, sex with James was phenomenal. I would go as far as to say, the best I had ever had. If I could only keep having sex with him without it affecting how I felt about him.
My only conclusion was to take sex back off the table, if only to protect my heart.

I was well and truly fucked otherwise!

JAMES

Yesterday had to have been the best day of my life. Spending most of it in bed with Belle. Last night was even better, I think we manage a couple of hours sleep in between fucking and doing other stuff. Namely me sucking and licking and tongue fucking that delicious pussy of hers. We couldn't get enough of each other.
I know that sex wasn't part of out marriage contract, but fuck, am I glad we decided to give in to temptation and go for it. This so-called marriage of convenience is the best idea I have come up with because, it get's me Belle and I know that over time while we are married, I can get her to fall in love with me and make our marriage a reality.
I practically skipped my way to the new offices to check everything was going as it should be.
Kenny Bradford, my partner in crime was already there when I arrived.

'Hey Kenny, how are things going?' I look around the space and see that all the furniture is in place. Kenny is sorting through files on top of the filing cabinet and turns to me when he hears my voice.

'James. It's going great. Everything is finished, just these files to sort and we are ready for the grand opening. Well except...' He paused.

'Except what?'

'We need a receptionist or are we going to do everything ourselves?' He raised a questioning brow.

'Shit! With everything going on, I completely forgot about that, sorry buddy. Look, get in touch with an agency and get them to send a temp to start on Monday until we can advertise for someone more permanent'.

'Sounds like a plan. So, what are you up to now? Do you fancy grabbing some lunch, I'm just about done here'. He started rubbing his tummy and grinning like a Cheshire cat. I laughed and nodded.

'Yeah, there is a place just down the road from here, they do a mean steak sandwich'.

'Ohh yes. Sold'.

Kenny locked up the office and we made our way down the street towards the Sandwich House. There was a small queue inside and we didn't have to wait long to be served. We grabbed a table by the window. It was warm, so I removed my suit jacket and rolled up my shirt sleeves before tucking in to my steak sandwich.
I watched Kenny bite in to his and moan.

'It's good isn't it?' I nodded to his sandwich.

THE SEXY FAKER

'Fuck. I think I am in love with this sandwich. In fact, I may have just come a little in my pants'. He grinned and took another large bite.

Laughing at his ridiculousness, I turned my head to see Belle across the street walking in the opposite direction and then entering a building that I knew to be a lap dancing aka strip joint.

WHAT THE FUCK!

Why the hell was she going in there?

I dropped my food on the table and stood up abruptly, knocking the chair over.

'James? What's wrong? You look like you've seen a ghost'.

I knew my face had a murderous look on it because I felt it, and I couldn't help it. All I could think was that Belle was so desperate after getting fired from her job at the law firm, that she was now looking for work as a stripper or lap dancer. Over my dead fucking body!

'I just remembered something I need to do. I'll catch you later'. I rush out of there and across the street to the building where Belle inside.

My pulse is racing. My chest tight. Clenching my fists, I pull the door open and go inside. It was dark and dingy, low lighting as you would expect in a place like this. I waited a few seconds to allow my eyes to adjust to the darkness, then made my way further in to the room.

I couldn't see anyone, but as I rounded a corner, I could hear muted voices coming from my left. I edged my way in that direction. There were two females and a male voice. They seemed to be arguing back and forth. I knew that neither one of the female voices I heard was Belle, so I moved on further down that hallway towards an open door where I could hear more voices. The one female voice I recognised to be Belles, she was talking to a man. I froze to the spot when I heard the conversation.

'You need to push it in, then pull it out Brenden'. She whined.

'What? No way, are you crazy?'

'Look, you know how much I need it. Now, are you going to co-operate with me or not? Because I don't think Vivian is going to like it if you don't'.

'Fine. Let's get it over with so I can get back to work'.

The next thing I hear is something rattling and banging. Are they fucking against something? You have got to be kidding me! When I heard a groan and a grunt, I had heard enough and lost my shit. My nostrils flaring and baring my teeth, I charge in to the room, swinging the door wide. Cracking my knuckles, as the door banged on the wall, ready to punch the dirty bastard that has his grubby hands on my Belle. I am fucking fuming. A red mist has covered my eyes. All I see is him next to my Belle.

'James?' Belle's puzzled frown almost stops me.

'Get your fucking hands off her now' I grind out and take another step forward. My hands fisting at my thighs.
Belle walks over to me and peers up at me through long dark

lashes. She touches my arm. I hadn't even noticed she had moved.

'James. What are you doing here? I thought I was seeing you tonight?'

Her calming voice made me turn my head to look down at her face. Her beautiful eyes piercing through me.
When I looked back over at the man, it was then that I noticed what was going on. That the scene I entered on to was innocent. And of the mistake I had made.
There had been no touching. No sexual contact at all. I was an idiot. I had no valid reason for thinking she would do something so dirty. No reason not to trust her, and I hang my head in shame.

'Belle, I …'. I didn't know what to say to her. An apology seemed rather pathetic at this point. Still, I had to know what they had been doing, if only for my own sanity.

'James, why are you here? Did you follow me?'

'What? No, I wouldn't do that. I saw you from across the street, I was having lunch with a colleague and … well I wondered why you would be coming in to this kind of … erm … establishment. So, I … why are you in here and what the hell did I walk in on Belle?' I raised my eyebrow at her now. She looked back at that Brenden bloke then at me again. Shaking her head in disbelief at my words. She took a step back and smiled widely. Even though you could see she was trying to contain the laughter dying to burst out.

'James. Did you think I had come here to dance or strip, maybe?' She looked behind her again at Brenden, who was now leaning against the tall filing cabinet that they had both been at, when I had first walked in. To say he had an amused look on his face would be an understatement. The smug fucker! I still would like to smash his face in. Yeah, I could easily take him on. He was about the same height as me slightly smaller build than me. I could definitely take him. Instead, I cleared my throat, because fuck ...yeah, I was embarrassed, and it must have shown on my goddamn face, because I sure as hell felt it. The burning sensation rising up from my chest to my neck and face. I scrubbed a hand over my face hoping to wipe it away, though knowing it wouldn't do any good, I just needed to do something to distract for a second. To try and compose myself.

'Just tell me Belle. Please, I beg of you'. I don't think I have begged anyone for anything in my entire life.

'Fine. I'll put you out of the misery you seem to be in. I got a call for my services as a lawyer. One of the girls here is in need of my help. Brenden here, is supposed to give me the file on a client of this ... establishment ... only the stupid draw is stuck, and well, we were trying to get the damn thing open when you walked ... I mean ... barged in here making your demands'. She had the gall to quirk a brow at me.
The relief that washed over me was immense to say the least. My heart rate went back to normal and my red face subsided. I knew the scene I had walked in on, had been innocent. The fact was, I had been blinded with rage and

jealousy and didn't see what was in front of me. Her hands flat against the draw of the filing cabinet, obviously pushing at it. His hand holding on to the handle of said draw and trying to pull it open. To have her confirmation was a weight off my shoulders, and I let out a breath I hadn't realised I had been holding.

'Right. I see that' I mumbled. Then a little louder. 'Well, I guess I should go then, leave you to it. I have stuff to get back to myself. We're still on for dinner, tonight right? Unless I have totally messed this up'. I feel a lump in my throat and my mouth is dry. I have fucked up big time, I just hope she doesn't shun me now. My heart is pounding so hard, it feels about to jump from my chest. The anticipation of her answer is slowly killing me, so I close my eyes and take a deep breath. Waiting. It seems like forever before she answers.

'Yes James, dinner is still on'.

'Great. I'll pick you up at seven thirty'. I spun on my heel and hurried out of there, because I knew if I had stayed any longer, I would have made an even bigger fool out of myself than I already had done.

I knocked on her door at seven twenty-five. I had sat outside in my car for the last twenty minutes, because pacing at my place just wasn't cutting it. I had cursed myself for the rest of today after I had left her at that strip club. How stupid I had been to think that she would do something so low to earn money. I could have easily lost her today and that wasn't

anything I was willing to do. Not now that this plan of mine was working. I just had to keep myself and my thoughts in check, at least until after the wedding, then all bets were off. I would work damn hard to make her fall in love with me.
I stand there waiting for the door to open, almost in a daze, my sweaty palms the only evidence of my nerves trying to get the better of me.
The door opens slowly and there she is standing before me like the goddess she is. My goddess.
The emerald green dress that stops just above her knees, makes the blue in her eyes pop brighter than ever before. Her barely their make-up and up-do make her look classy. My beautiful, stunning Belle. She takes my breath away.
I hadn't realised she had spoken until she nudges me in the ribs.

'Sorry, what?'

'I said, where are we going, or is it a surprise?'

'We're going to a place called Fortuna. Have you been before?'

'Yeah, with Ricky. The food there is to die for. Thank you for taking me James'. She grabs her clutch bag and edges out of the door, locking it.
I offer my arm to her and she wraps her small delicate hand around it, as we make our way out.
After settling in to the car, I turn to her and cup her cheek.
'I'm sorry about earlier today. I shouldn't have assumed you would stoop to those levels. My initial reaction was un-called

for and I apologise. I hope you can forgive me and that it doesn't spoil our plans'.

The blank expression on her face unnerves me, because I couldn't read what she was thinking or feeling.

'Sure, of course, James. I wouldn't want anything to spoil ... your plans'. The coldness in her eyes and her voice, made me wince and jerk my hand away from her face. It also caused a tightness in my chest and my mouth go so dry, I had to swallow a few times to moisten my throat and tongue, so I could speak without croaking.

'Ok'.

'Ok'.

We drove in silence all the way to the restaurant and it was putting me on edge. I hated it. Something was off with her. She seemed to have forgiven me earlier, so I know that wasn't it. But I couldn't get my head around what could be wrong with her. Maybe she will tell me later. Maybe it's because she's just hangry. Yeah, feeding her will help matters and lighten the mood. I hoped anyway.

THE SEXY FAKER

ANNABELLE

The nerve of him! I knew for sure now that all I was to him was a convenience. A way for him to keep his damn company. Ricky had been right about James after all. I couldn't wait for all this to be over.
At least I would have my own room at his place, so I could live my own life outside of this stupid marriage deal.
To think that I could have been so stupid as to think he cared anything for me. When he had gone all alpha on me at the lap dancing club earlier, I felt for sure it was because he had feelings for me, that maybe he did love me. More than just friends, how wrong I was about that! I won't be letting the jerk fool me again, that's for sure.
I could hardly speak to him tonight at the restaurant, and when he dropped me back at my place, I made it clear that I was tired and just needed my bed ... alone. He kissed my cheek and stared at me for what seemed like hours. His eyes bored in to mine. Searching, looking, for what I don't know, but I am pretty sure he realised at some point, that I was pissed at him. Then he left, and it felt like he had ripped my heart out and taken it with him, all over again.
So, here I am, laying in my cold and lonely bed and feeling

sorry for myself. I stopped doing pity parties years ago. So why was I doing this to myself. It's not like he knows that he has hurt me. He's too damn blind to see it for a start. All he see's is his best friend, doing him a big favour. So why can't I just see it for what it is?
Why can't I see that I am being his friend and help him? Why can't he see that I am more than just his best friend? That he is more to me?
Why am I constantly asking myself the same damn questions over and over, when I already the answers?
Arrgh! I grab the pillow from under my head and thump it a few times, before throwing it across the room. Yeah, I was having a tantrum which made me fucked up, I know. Thank god no-one could see me as I flung myself out of bed and began stomping around the bedroom, picking up anything that was in front of me and throwing it against the wall.
Tears poured down my face before I realised, and my blood was boiling. I kept going until all the energy drained out of me and I collapsed against my chest of drawers.
How the fuck was I going to protect my heart when I was already hurting?
My bedroom was a wreck and now so was I.

I woke up still on the bedroom floor. I must have cried myself to sleep last night. I groaned when I saw the state of my room.
I had to be at the lap dancing club again today to talk to the young woman about the assault she endured from one of the patrons. The last thing I wanted to do was walk in their

THE SEXY FAKER

feeling and looking like I did at the moment.
A cool shower should take the edge off. I wasn't going to think about James today, I would have to deal with him soon enough tomorrow night at the opening party.
By the time I got back from the club, after hours upon hours of talking to my client and getting some semblance of a plan of action together, I was tired but satisfied that I could win the case against that scumbag that had attacked one of their employees.
I showered and changed in to yoga pants and a oversized sweater, I didn't even bother putting a bra or panties back on, before making some pasta and garlic bread.
I was about to sit down to eat, when there was a knock at my door. I checked the time. Six o'clock. I knew it couldn't be Ricky, he was at work by now. So, it could only be James. The one person I wasn't ready to see yet.
Sighing heavily, I dragged myself off the sofa and went to answer the door.
James stood there looking sheepish as I took in his appearance. He was dressed in a dark grey three-piece suit with a crisp white shirt and black tie. He looked like he had just walked off a men fashion magazine.
Why the hell did he have to be so damn good looking and make me swoon every time I see him. It was so unfair for him to be that way and make my lady bits swoon along with me. When my eyes finally reached his, he was smirking. My face and neck reddened at been caught perusing him from the feet up.

THE SEXY FAKER

'What are you doing here James?'

'I came to give you this'.
It was then that I noticed he had a large pink box, fastened with black ribbon, in his hand.

'What is that?'

'It's for the party tomorrow. I saw it and immediately thought of you'. He walked past me and placed the box on the sofa.

'James, you really didn't have to buy me gifts and especially for the party. I have dresses of my own I can wear'.
He stalked over to me and took my hands in to his.

'I know I don't have to buy you anything Belle. I wanted to. Open it and see what is inside. I know you will love it'.
I sighed heavily and began to untie the ribbon. I removed the lid and lifted the tissue paper inside. A small gasp escaped me.
Lifting the dress out of the box, I hold it up against my body and grinned.

'James, this dress is beautiful. But, I can't accept it, I'm sorry'.
I shake my head and lay the dress back in the box.

'What? Of course, you can accept It. Belle, the dress matches your eyes and when I saw it, I knew it was perfect for you. Wear it tomorrow night for the party'.

'So, now you are telling me what I should wear. Is this what it will be like married to you James? Running my life for me?'
The disdain in my tone is palpable.

'What? Of, course not. Why on earth would you think that Belle? I would never tell you what to do. Look, if the dress bothers you that much, then don't wear it. I just wanted to do something nice for you, that's is all. There is no agenda here Belle, I promise'.

'Ok, thank you. So, is this what you came here for, to bring me the dress?'

He lifts his hands and cups my cheeks. Lowering his head towards me and placing a soft kiss to my lips.

'Not just the dress'. He whispers on my lips. He deepens the kiss then and I can't help myself and melt in to arms. One of his hands wraps around my hair, while the other caresses my hip.
'Belle'.

'James'.

He moves us backwards until my legs hit the sofa and he gently lays me down. Moving on top of me, his hands touching my body like he can't get enough of me.
I shouldn't be doing this. I can't be doing this. But maybe just one last time, then I will tell him that sex is off the table. That we need to stick to the plan and keep it just business. I know he'll understand because it is his plan after all to save his position in the company and sex was never part of that plan. It was just something we fell in to.
I let out a little moan as his lips move down my neck. His hands are now at the hem of my top and lifting it up. He finds my breast and squeezes gently before running his thumb

over my now hard nipple and his arousal evident as he pushes his hard erection against my centre. Rubbing at my swollen bud.
He pulls my top up and over my head and latches his mouth on to my nipple. Licking and flicking, suckling on it, the sensation making the heat between my legs needier.

'Belle, you always taste so good. I need to taste more of you right now'. He moved down my body slowly, tugging at the waist band of my yoga pants and pulling them down. Kissing down my stomach towards the apex of my thighs, my pants are removed altogether.

'Fuck, Belle. No underwear? Do you know how hot that is and how hard you make me?' His voice is hoarse with lust.

He glides his fingers across my already glistening lips and pushes one inside of me.

'You are already wet for me. That is so fucking sexy'.

He pumps in to me a few times before lowering his head and touching the tip of his tongue to my clit. I almost jump off the sofa at the sensation. His finger continues to pound away. When he adds another finger and then another, my back arches up as the orgasm hits me. I am panting like I have just run a marathon. I look down and see his smiling face. His chin and lips are shiny with my juices.
I watch him stand and take out his wallet, removing a condom. When he is sheathed, he lays back over and lifts one of my legs up and drapes it over the back of the sofa, then pushes my other knee up to my chest.

THE SEXY FAKER

He positions himself at my entrance and slowly enters me, causing us both to gasp.

'Jesus, you feel so fucking good Belle. I don't think I will ever get enough of you'.

My pussy clenched. He withdraws, only for him to drive forward again and again. He takes one of my nipples in to his mouth as he continues to ram inside of me.
I dig my nails in to his butt cheeks, urging him to thrust deeper in to me. His hips grind against mine as I drag my nails over his ass and up his back. He hisses and picks up speed. His thrusts growing stronger and deeper. I clutch on tight, our bodies crushed together as my walls clamp on his length like a vice. He groans, losing himself in me, his head falling back, his body trembling as he releases every last ounce in to me.
The only sounds in the room now are of us panting, trying to catch our breath.
James pulled out of me and went to the bathroom to dispose of the condom. When he came back I was still laying there. He lifted my legs up, sat down, then lowered them on to his lap, where he started to massage my calf muscles. I couldn't help the low moan leave my lips.

'God, that feels so good'. It did too, I could lay here for the rest of the night letting him do that.

'Anything for you Belle. Remember that'.
But did he really mean it? Or was he just saying it because he felt he had to? Because of the stupid marriage plan!

THE SEXY FAKER

I removed my legs from his lap and sat up, feeling a little self-conscious, I grab my yoga pants off the floor and stand up, holding them in front of me.

'I should get dressed and I think it is time you left now James. I need some space. What time will you be picking me up for the party tomorrow?'
With a stony expression, his lips tighten in to thin line. His voice drops as he replies.

'Be ready for seven o'clock'. He dresses quickly and as he reaches the door to leave he pauses.
I straighten by spine, waiting to hear what he has to say and dreaded it. But he shakes his head then opens the door, closing it quietly behind him.
I dropped back down on the sofa and bury my face in my hands, because now I just feel like shit. Like a whore who just had sex then kicked him out.
What the hell was wrong with me?
I loved him, so why the hell was I treating him like crap?
Oh, yeah, that's right. He doesn't love me back. I was trying to protect my heart. Trouble was, I was hurting my heart all by myself.

THE SEXY FAKER

JAMES

I couldn't believe she threw me out like that! What the hell did I do to deserve that kind of treatment? I thought we were getting somewhere too. I knew she had been pissed at me for whatever reason and that was why I had bought her the dress. To at least try and make it up to her. I didn't understand what I had done wrong. She said she needed space, so I will give it to her. until tomorrow that is.
As I stepped outside the building my phone buzzed with a text from Richard.

RICH- hey I got a call from some bird called Davina says she's your fiancée care to explain before Annabelle hears about it & how the fuck did she even get my number?

Fuck! That bitch just won't give up. She is like a fucking leech! My limit is now reached, as soon as I text Richard back, I'm calling my lawyers and getting her destroyed.

JAMES- DEFFO AN EX BRO THAT BITCH JUST CAN'T LET GO CALLING MY LAWYERS RIGHT NOW & I HAVE NO IDEA HOW SHE GOT YOUR NUMBER

THE SEXY FAKER

RICH- ok but watch your back she is here & I think she's after more than you

JAMES- THANKS WILL KEEP THAT IN MIND

The bitch is here? What the fuck! Maybe I should find her and see what the hell she want's. All this fiancée business is going to fuck up my plans and fuck up everything I am building with Belle. I will not let Davina ruin this for me. Whatever scheme she has cooked up, I will make sure to destroy not only her plans but her too.
I take out my phone and remember I was going to block her. did I do it? Shit! I won't be able to call her if I did and I don't know her number off hand. I panic for a split second as I scroll through my contacts, letting out a sigh of relief when I see it.
I press call and wait. Her drawling voice when she picks up, makes me grind my jaw.

'Darling, so good to hear from you'.

'Cut the crap Davina and tell me what you want'.

'Why James, you already know what I want'.

'Nope. Not happening. I have told you already to leave me alone, and now you are bothering my brother with your shit'.

'James, we both know you will come back to me. You always come back to me. We are so damn good together and you know it'.

THE SEXY FAKER

Fucking hell! The gall of this woman knew no bounds. 'Stop it. Just fucking stop it. I will be contacting my lawyers and getting a restraining order put on your ass …'.

'Good, at least you won't get anywhere near the baby'.

Baby? What the hell is she on about now!

'Davina, I don't know what game you are playing, but it needs to stop now …'.

'No games James. You are going to be a daddy, so unless you never want to see your child, you will give me what I want'.

I staggered back at her words. She couldn't be serious? Me, a dad? No fucking way. It had to be one of her manipulations and I wasn't going to keep going around this merry go round with her. I needed her out of my life before she did any damage between me and Belle.

'James? Are you still there? If you heard what I just said, then make it happen. Today. I am at the Grenada Hotel room 555. Be here in two hours'.

The bitch rang off before I had chance to say anything. But what could I say? She held all the cards at this moment in time. I was still dazed and confused about this baby she kept going on about.
She kept going on about me knowing what she wanted. To give her what she wanted! She is fucking crazy if she thinks I would ever take her back. Nope, definitely not happening. So, whatever this stupid idea she has about me having a child, she can kiss my ass, because I know for sure that I have

never impregnated any woman. I have always practiced safe sex. Always covered my cock with a condom. Never gone bare back with anyone. So, whatever or whoever she has paid to lie, (because that is the only obvious answer) and say she is carrying my child, I will destroy them too.

I can't have any of this getting back to Belle. Yeah, I know my next plan of action is probably not the best idea, but I am going to the hotel to see that bitch, and I am not waiting two hours either. I will make her tell me who the woman is, saying I have a child with her, and then get her out of my life, once and for all.

I take a deep breath and gather myself. The last thing I want to do is go in their all guns blazing and messing this up.

I get in my car and begin making my way to the hotel. She is in for one hell of shock, when I turn up at her door.

Outside the hotel room door, I take a deep breath, count to ten then knock, loudly.

When the door swings open, I am shocked to see Davina sporting a swollen belly. She must have seen it on my face too because when I eventually looked at her face, she was smirking.

'Well hello, James. You're early, but then I guess it is you and you have to do things right away don't you? That has always been a fault of yours you know. Please come in, this is a conversation for us only'.

Still stunned and I guess in shock, at seeing her this way, I followed her in to the room and dropped down on to one of the couches. Placing my head in my hands. My chest

tightened as I felt her sit next to me.
This could not be happening. Not now. Not with everything going to plan with Belle.

'How far along are you?' I couldn't even look at her.

'In case you are wondering, yes, the baby is yours and I am just six months as of last week'.

I looked up at her then, only to see her still smirking at me. She really was a piece of work. If she thinks she can trap me in to being with her, marrying her even, she had another thing coming!
I levelled her with a stare. 'If that baby is mine, which I very much doubt, then I need a DNA doing to determine. I will then set up a child support agreement. But know this Davina, I will not nor will ever, take you back. Do I make myself clear?'

She placed one of her well-manicured hands on my thigh and began to stroke. I tried not flinch, but it was impossible not to. I detested her touch, I detested everything about her.

'James' she giggled. Her hand moving further up until her fingers brushed against my crotch. Thank fuck my cock detested her too.
'James, the only thing I want from you, is you. Do I make myself clear? There will be no other negotiations'.

'What if I don't Davina? What the fuck do you think you can do that would ever have me take you back?'

THE SEXY FAKER

'I know the board members have given you a stipulation otherwise they will kick you out. I know you have some plan concocted to marry some whore, just so you can give them what you want. But I see it this way, with me now carrying your child, we should be the ones to get married. After all, isn't that what the board want, you settled down?'

I stood up abruptly. She has no fucking idea how much I could damage her reputation. She was a model and I could make jobs disappear with the click of my fingers.
If she thinks for one second, she has me cornered, then more fool her. I was done here. Done with her and her vindictiveness. She can try and blackmail all she wants, but I would destroy her, and if that child she is carrying is mine, then I will get custody. No child of mine would be brought up by someone as evil as her.

'You are crazy if you think you can blackmail me Davina. I am already engaged, and it is to someone I am in love with. So, do your worst, because I am telling you right now, anymore of your schemes and I will destroy you'.

I stormed towards the door swung the door open.

'Destroy is your favourite word isn't it James. But I can destroy you just the same'.

I didn't stop. I kept walking, because there was nothing she could do or say, that could destroy me.
I needed a drink. I take out my phone and call Richard.

'Hey bro, did you sort everything out?'

'Yeah, kind of. Right now, I could use a drink though, are you free?'

'Yeah, I'll meet you at Dooleys. I'm on my way'.

I hung up and jumped in my car. Dooleys was our place. It used to be a café but now it was a wine bar come eatery. I managed to find a parking space right out front and when I looked through the window, I could see Richard already sat at the bar. It was actually a relief to see him waiting for me already, because I would have probably downed a few drinks until he had arrived otherwise.

'Hey'. I say and slide on to the seat next to him at the bar.

'Ok, bro. Who the fuck is this Davina bitch and why is she calling me? What gives and what about Annabelle if she finds out?'

'I need a drink first before I go in to that'. I order a JD on the rocks and take a big gulp before I wipe my mouth and face my brother.
'Davina is this model I was seeing back in L.A. I broke it off with her months ago, but she won't leave me alone'.

'Right. First of all, if she is a model she must me hot as fuck. Second, why the hell would dump that?'

'Because she is crazy. I put up with her shit for months. She may be a model, but she is not a nice person. I mean, she totally berates anyone who didn't pander to her. A total fucking diva and manipulator. It was the last straw when I caught her red-handed cheating on me with someone from

THE SEXY FAKER

my office. I had tried many a time to break things off with her, but she knew how to get to me. Used sex as fucking weapon on me and of course it worked every time. There is no denying she is gorgeous. But the cheating was what finally made me realise I needed to be away from her for good'. I take another large gulp of my drink, finishing it off. Catching the barman's attention, I ordered another one.

'Hey, take it easy on those, will you. I don't want to have to carry your drunken arse out of here. Ok, so why is she here if you ended it with her? what does she want?'

'Me. That's what she wants. She is also pregnant and saying it is mine. I doubt it though, because I always suited up and when I caught her fucking that prick I know for a fact he wasn't wearing anything. So, the baby is probably his or some other sad fucker who had the misfortune of shagging her'.

Richard lets out a long whistle. 'What are you going to do?'

'Nothing. I told her before I accept the baby as mine I need a DNA test doing. Then, and only then, will discuss options with her and that none of them would be me taking her back'.

'Brutal. What did she say to that?'

'That she would destroy me'. I slam the glass down on the counter.

'Fuck! Can she do that?'

'Nope, she has got nothing on me that could or would destroy me. I told her to do her worst'.

THE SEXY FAKER

'Wow James, look. I know what she said is probably bullshit, to make you squirm and all that. But, and I learned this the hard way, never underestimate a woman scorned. Just be careful, ok, and don't forget I am here, whatever you need'.

'Thanks, and I have nothing to be careful about. There is nothing she can do or say that will hurt me. So, don't worry. I need to get home and sort some stuff out for tomorrow. You're still coming right, to the opening party?'

'Wouldn't miss it for the world bro. Catch you later'. The big lump jumps off his stool and grabs me in a bear hug, patting my back hard for good measure.

ANNABELLE

I put the dress on and looked at myself for far too long in the mirror. The dress looked amazing on me. Fit like a glove. He definitely has a perfect eye for women's dresses. Shit! Now I start wondering how many dresses he has bought for other women! Keeping my feelings intact is harder than I anticipated and after the wedding, it is only going to get harder.
I take my shoes out the box and manage to get one on as the doorbell chimes. I hop down the hall and look through the peephole. James, and he is early. Typical!
I open the door and make my way back towards my bedroom to get my other shoe.

'You not ready yet, hop a long Cassidy?' He arches a brow at me in question.

Yeah, I may have just given him my middle finger as I closed the bedroom door. I will be ready when I am ready and not before. End of.
When I finally appear ten minutes later, he is sat on the sofa looking through his phone. He looks up at me and then peruses my body from top to toe, then back up again. All the

while with a big grin on his face. He stands up and walks over until we are toe to toe and I have to look up at him.

'You are beautiful'. He almost whispers, then cupping my face, he bends down and lightly brushes his lips to mine. I can't help it, I let out a little groan. My body obviously didn't get the memo, the traitor, about me taking sex off the table with James. I need to stop this now, before he takes it any further and we end up having sex before we leave the apartment.

'James. We should go'. I take a step back away from him and grab my clutch bag off the coffee table and head to the door.

'Yes, of course. When we get there, I will introduce you to the board and remember they already think we are engaged. I guess I should give you this'.

He pulls a blue velvet box out of his inside pocket and opens it up. Inside is the most gorgeous ring I have ever seen. It looks vintage, antique even. Emeralds and diamonds glitter in the light.

'Wow, that is so beautiful James. Where did you get it? I mean, I promise I will take care of it until I have to give it back when the marriage is over, sorry'. I winched slightly at my own words and looking at him, I think he may have too.

'No, you're right, of course. Here, let me put it on you'. He lifts my left hand and slides the ring on to my finger. Holding it there, he takes a deep breath, closing his eyes.

'James, are you ok?'

THE SEXY FAKER

His eyes pop back open and he smiles. Rubbing the back of my hand with his thumb.
'Yes. I guess we should get going'.

When we get outside, there is a limo waiting by the curb. I glance back at him and smirk.
'Arriving in style hey. Me likey'. I giggle and climb inside. James slides in next to me.

'Only the best for you Belle. Would you like a drink?' he opens the mini bar and takes out a miniature bottle of champagne and pours us both a glass.

'What shall we toast to'. I ask.

'How about, to new beginnings'. We clink our glasses, and both take a sip.

Twenty minutes later we arrive at the venue where the party is being held. There are already people milling about as we get out of the limo. James takes a hold of my hand and gently squeezes it, when he sees me shiver.

'You'll be fine. Stop fretting, you got this, and I got you'. He winks then steers me up the steps and inside.
The party is in full swing. Music is playing. Everyone is drinking. People are standing at the bar waiting to be served. Most of them look like stuffed shirts. Not my kind of people, even if I am a lawyer.

'Come with me. Luck would have it that the board seem to have congregated together over there in that far corner'. He leads the way towards a table where four men and four women are seated having somewhat of a heated discussion. One of the men happened to look up as we approached and stood up to greet us.

'James, good to see you and this lovely lady must Belle, is that right?'

'Yes, pleased to meet you'. I held out my hand for him to shake, but instead of taking it, he grabbed me in to a bear hug.

'Trevor, for heavens sake, put the girl down. I am so sorry Belle, please excuse my husband. He's a little rough around the edges but he's harmless. I'm Margie, why don't the two of you have a seat'.

James pulls a chair out for me then takes the one next to me while Trevor does the introductions.

'That big lump over there is Jason and Patricia next to him his wife. This is Eric and his wife Donna and next to James is Walter and his wife Janet'.

We all say hello's and then Trevor asks a passing waitress for more Champagne. I don't miss the look she gives James when she leans over between us to collect the empty glasses and her breasts brush against his arm. I look at James, but he seems to be oblivious to her flirting and instead is having a discussion about number increases or something, I have no clue about. But I can't help the small smile that twitches on my lips.

'He has that effect on all women, dear. Don't think for one second that he will stray. I see the way he looks at you and there is love there'. Margie patted my hand, smiling and took a sip of her Champagne.

'Oh, I'm not worried at all Margie, but thanks'. I looked back at James who was now looking at me and smiling.

'Everything ok Belle?' he slid his hand around the back of my chair. His thumb brushing the bare skin of my back.

'Yes, everything is ok James'.
The band on stage played a slow song and James stood, holding out his hand.

'May I have this dance?'
I took his hand and he led me towards the dance floor. He placed a hand on the small of my back and held me close to his hard chest.

'You look beautiful tonight Belle. I couldn't imagine doing any of this with anyone else. Look, there is something I want to say and if I don't say it now, I think I might burst but … I don't want to waste any more time pretending I don't know what I want. Because I do know … it's you Belle, it has always been you'.

'But …'.

'I don't want to hear any but's Belle, because excuses and doubts have never done anything but come between us. I want to make up for the time we lost. I want to wake up next to you every morning and to kiss you goodnight every night. I want to make love to you and worship your body every day. I want to eat breakfasts and dinners with you. Belle, I want everything with you'. He cups my face and wipes the stray tear from my cheek.

'James I …'.

'I am in love with you Belle. I have been since we were kids. It has always been you'.
He lowered his head, his kiss stealing my breath away, but his words damn near made my heart stop beating.
I can't believe the words that came out of his mouth. They were the last words I expected to hear from him. But I can see the emotion in his eyes and I can hear the truth in his words. I can't stop the tears from falling. My lips tremble as I reach up and put a shaky hand against his cheek.
He had been so honest with me that something inside me had cracked. The wall around my heart came tumbling down and I realised I had to be as honest with him as he had been with me.

'I love you too James, so very much. I have always loved you'. I whispered against his lips.
He pulled me in even tighter and crashed his lips to mine in a kiss so exquisite and deep, that I could hardly breathe and the people around us disappeared as we devoured each other.
James eventually ended the kiss and placed his forehead against mine. Both of us breathing heavily.

'I guess that makes us a couple for real Belle'. He chuckled then grabbed my hand. 'Come on, let's get back to the table and eat something before I drag you home and fuck you until you can't walk'.

'Such a romantic James. No wonder you have women falling at your feet'. He pulled me to his side and kissed my temple and I couldn't help the wide goofy grin on my face.

'I only have eyes for you Belle'.
When we reached our table, there was a woman sat in my seat with her back to me. I didn't think anything of it until I felt James stiffen and saw his back straighten.

'James, what is it?' I didn't know what to think, but I knew it had something to do with the woman sat at our table, and then she stood up and turned to face us, sneering at me. She looked me up and down and stuck her nose in the air.
It was at that moment I noticed she was sporting a swollen tummy. She was pregnant, but who was she to James?

'James darling, I have been waiting forever'.

'Davina, what the hell are you doing here?'

I looked between the two of them. James had let go of my hand and was clenching his fists.
Trevor stood up abruptly and glared at James, throwing his napkin down on his plate.

'James, what is the meaning of this? Ms Boothright here tells me that you are already engaged to her and are having a baby. Is this some kind of sick joke? She has travelled all the way from L.A in her condition and all you have to say for yourself is "what the hell are you doing here?" and what

about Belle. From the look on her face, she had no idea about any of this either. This is unacceptable behaviour James and we will be discussing this back at the office on Monday. Now, maybe you should escort your "real" fiancée home and make sure Belle here gets home safely too. I expect you have some explaining to do young man'.
James jaw clenched, his cheek ticked as he tried to hold his composure in front of the board members. But I couldn't stand there any longer.
Before I could think or see what James or Davina was going to do or say. I spun on my heel and high tailed it out of there. The last thing I wanted was for anyone to see my snotty tear stained face and I luckily found a taxi the minute I exited the building.
There was no stopping the cascade of tears streaming down my face. The taxi driver eyed me through his rear-view mirror and asked if I was ok. 'I will be, thank you'. I replied, because what else could I say? That the man who I loved and had professed his love to me, was already engaged to be married to another woman who was having his baby? I didn't even want to think about it, let alone say it out loud.
I couldn't help myself and looked through the back window as the taxi set off. A man ran out of the double glass doors and watched me drive away. But it wasn't James who came after me, no. It was Ricky, my dear faithful friend. I wondered if he knew about this woman Davina and the baby she was carrying? He had lied to me before. Kept things from me. Why wouldn't he say anything about his brother's fiancée and the baby, if he had known? Why wouldn't James for that

matter. Why on earth could he come up with this plan of his, if he was already engaged anyway?

The board wouldn't have had to threaten him.

None of it made any sense.

What game was he playing?

And why the hell would he involve me in it?

JAMES

My blood was boiling. My body shook with rage at the sight of Davina. What the fuck was she doing here?
By the look on my board members faces sat at the table, it was clear that she had spouted her venom about me being the father of her unborn child. The bitch had no right to interfere with my life like this.
Trevor's little speech left me reeling and as I spun around to speak to Belle, my heart sunk when I realised she was nowhere to be seen.
Davina slinked up beside me, wrapping her talons around my forearm and leaned in to whisper in my ear.

'Darling, why don't we take a seat. Forget about that little tart and enjoy our evening together'.

Gritting my teeth, I grabbed her wrist and removed her clutch from my arm. My eyes bore in to hers as I spoke. Making sure my voice was low enough that only she could hear it.

'Don't ever touch me again. Belle is hundred times the woman you'll ever wish to be. Now why don't you make some excuse and fuck off'.

THE SEXY FAKER

The only thing I wanted to do right now was to find Belle. I had to try and explain the Davina situation to her and get her to understand.
I excused myself from the table, telling them I was going to the men's room, then made my way towards the exit. I searched the room as I went and even asked a woman who was entering the ladies room if she would see if Belle was in there, after giving her a description of her. When the lady came back out and declared no-one fitting that description was in there, I took off to the foyer, hoping to catch her.
I ran in to Richard instead.

'Richard, has Belle come through here?' I panted, resting my hands on my knees after running up the flight of steps two at a time that ascended to the foyer.

'Yeah, she went rushing by as I came out of the men's room. I called out to her, but she didn't hear me ... come to think of it, she looked upset ... what the hell have you done now brother?'

'Fucking Davina is here. I need to catch Belle and explain to her. I was about to but when I turned around, she was gone'.
I started to run towards the exit when Richards voice stopped me.

'No James. I will go, seeing you right now won't stop her from running. She's hurting, give her some space. Let me go find her. I'll let you know she's ok'.
I let out a heavy sigh, because I knew he was right. Me chasing after Belle now, will only make her stubborn ass push

me away, and that was the last thing I wanted her to do.
I honestly can't believe how I have fucked up, again. I am my own worst enemy sometimes.

'Ok, I guess I had better go back and try to explain to the board about the Davina situation. That is if she hasn't already fucked me over with them'. Shaking me head, Richard patted me on the back.

'Bro, we got this. That bitch won't get away with attempting to ruin your life and once Belle know everything, she will understand and support you too'.

'I'm not so sure, but thanks Richard. it means a lot for you having my back. Now go see that Belle is ok and let me know'.

I head back inside. There is no sign of Davina anywhere near the table, thank god. I just need to explain to Trevor and the rest of the guys about her and hopefully they won't follow through with there threat of kicking me out of my own company.

I make my way through the other tables and just before I get to mine, a hand touches my shoulder. When I spin around, Margie is looking up at me.

'Oh, hello Margie'. I lean down and kiss her cheek.

'James dear, please tell me that god awful woman is not telling the truth about you and her being engaged'.

Taking a deep breath, I look her straight in the eye, so she knows I am telling her the truth.

'Davina is not my fiancée. Never has been and never will be. Not that she doesn't want that. We had a fling months ago and I ended it when I caught her cheating on me. The baby she is carrying, she says is mine, but I don't believe her. I have requested a DNA test, but she is stalling … look, Belle is the woman I love and the only woman I want to marry. I didn't tell her about Davina and now I think … I think I have lost her and I don't know what to do'.

'Oh, James, you must tell Trevor what you have told me. You don't have to worry about what the board will do. It is clear to everyone how much you and Belle are in love. That Davina woman has no hope of getting you, no matter what she say's or tries to do to ingratiate herself with the board and their wives. Us wives had her sussed the minute she sat down. Now, don't you worry about a thing and go and be with your Belle. I will sort out Trevor'. She patted my cheek and left me standing there, stunned. By the sound of it, Margie and the other wives had some clout when it came to their husbands. Who knew!

I wasn't so sure about going to Belle's place, I didn't want to spook her, and I was still waiting for Richard to text me that she was ok. So, I went straight home instead and took a hot shower and put on some pyjama bottoms. Having missed the dinner at the party I quickly made myself a sandwich and got comfy on my large Italian leather sofa and waisted for Richards text.

I must have dozed off, because I awake with a jolt. The dream I had just had of Belle and Davina stabbing her in the back, literally, was so vivid, it felt real. I have sweat rolling down the side of my face.

My phone has fallen on the floor, I pick it up to check the time and see a text from Richard that had been sent three hours ago.

RICHARD – ALL GOOD BRO BELLE IS HOME & SAFE I TOLD HER TO HEAR YOU OUT SHE SEEMS CONFUSED SHE SAID TO RING HER TOMORROW I THINK YOU SHOULD TELL HER EVERYTHING TOO

I don't bother to text back because it is two thirty in the morning. Instead, I drag myself to bed and hope I can fall back asleep and not lay awake all night worrying about how Belle is going to take it, if I were to tell her everything as my brother suggested. Everything being, why I had left all those years ago. I want to tell her the truth, but I am a coward, a weak man who is scared of losing her because she thinks I am not enough or worthy enough of her.

I may have millions in the bank and millions more in investments, but none of that matters if I don't have Belle in my life. She doesn't care how much money I have or material things. She has a heart of gold and a lot of love to give. I just hope I will still be on the receiving end of that love. I need this marriage plan to work, so at least she will be mine and I hope that treating her like the queen she is, she will eventually see the real me and realise that I am worthy of her.

THE SEXY FAKER

ANNABELLE

I am watching the floor numbers slowly change as I ascend in the elevator. My palms are sweaty, and I can feel a dribble of sweat running down my spine. I am nervous at the confrontation that awaits me. But I am here to find out her side of things.

James called me this morning and I have arranged to meet with him tonight for dinner, to talk things over. I just hope we can sort this out. I love him more than anything and I now know that he loves me. But if this Davina woman is carrying his baby, then it makes our relationship more complicated. Thank god for Ricky. When he came to my place last night to check on me, I was a complete mess.

He cradled me in his arms and calmed me down before admitting he had just recently found out about Davina and her claims. He told me that James didn't believe a single word she said about the baby, and that I wasn't to believe a word she said about the engagement. That James had broken up with her before weeks before he left L.A to come back home. That I should listen to what he had to say.

So, I told Ricky to text James to call me in the morning. I also asked him if he knew how to get a hold of Davina and luckily, he still had her number in his call history from when she had phoned him before.

I needed to meet her and get her side of the story she was spouting to everyone. I saw the expressions on the board members faces last night and I was damned if she was going to ruin James. So, we came up with a plan. Ricky called her to ask to meet her at her hotel room, his excuse was, so he could get to know the mother of his future niece or nephew. Only it wouldn't be him showing up, it would be me. She fell for it hook, line and sinker. The meeting was for one o'clock. But I was too on edge and ended up arriving forty minutes early.

So, here I am, just two floors away from my destination and twitching with anxiety. Which is ridiculous considering I am a lawyer and have been in court rooms.

I take out my compact mirror to check my appearance. I am nothing like Davina. She is tall and beautiful with long black hair and dark eyes. I mean, she is a freaking model for crying out loud. No, wonder James picked her. I bet he could have any woman he wanted too. I bet he already as.

I sigh and put the compact back in to my bag as the doors open to the floor I need.

I exit and follow the sign to where her room is located. As I turn the corner I come to a stop, because there she is, leaning against the open door and kissing a man. She is stood in nothing but lingerie. Does the woman have no shame! The man grips her ass then moves away. When he does I get a full-frontal view of her and I am confused by what I see. Her stomach is flat. Yep, flat as a fucking pancake. I thought

she was what five, maybe six months pregnant, but she doesn't look pregnant at all …. Wait … of all the low life fucked up shit she could have pulled! What a lying conniving, deceitful bitch.
How could she do this to James? What the hell is she trying to achieve by it?
I need to know what her game is. My feet begin to carry me towards her. thankfully she doesn't see me right away and I manage to practically be in front of her before she see's me. Her eyes widen in shock, as she tries to close the door on me, but my foot manages to stop the door shutting completely. I barge in and slam it closed behind me.

'What the hell do you think you are doing? Get out of here, now!'
The bitch can yell at me all she wants, but I'm not going anywhere. Not until I know what the hell is going on.
I take in the room. The bed is messy, not surprising since I just saw a man leaving the room, they obviously just had sex. Clothes are discarded everywhere and on the chair is a what looks like one of those baby bump contraption things, you know, the ones that pregnant women get their other halves to wear, so they understand the concept of the weight of carrying a baby around for nine months.
This confirms it, the cow was lying about being pregnant. She is wanting something from James and I am going to find out what it is.

'Wow, you really are something else aren't you'. I shake my head and take a step towards her.

'Not another step. You stay away from me or I will ... I will call for security'. Davina moves backwards towards the bed, where the phone is sitting on the night stand.
I shake my head again and cross my arms over my chest.

'Look, Davina. Whatever you have planned for James, stops now. Do you understand? Otherwise, I am going to tell him about you faking being pregnant ... actually, you know what ... I think I will tell him ... unless ...' I tap my finger on my chin.

'Unless what ... what are you going to do? Tell me what you want?'
Davina is on edge. I can tell she is shitting herself. Scared of what I will do or say. All I want from her though is the truth, then I will make sure she slings her hook and never contacts James again. I only hope her little plan hasn't thwarted James plan to keep the board on side.

'Unless you tell me everything. I want to know what you wanted from James and why you pretended to be pregnant'. She let's out a huff and drops to the bed.

'I wanted him back, ok! I thought that if I was carrying his baby he would drop everything and come back to L.A to be with me'.
This woman was completely insane!

'How the hell did you think that would work? He's not stupid and at some point, when you were supposed to give birth, he would know there was no baby. Or, maybe even when he tried to touch you, he would have known. Are you really that stupid?'

'I don't know. I would have said I had a miscarriage or something, once we got back to L.A or something. At least he would be with me'.

'There are so many reasons that would never have happened. But the main one being, that he doesn't love you'.

'Who said anything about love, not me. Oh, if you think he loves you sweetheart, then you are deluded. That man doesn't know how to love anyone, he's not even capable of it. I suggest you get out while you can honey, before you get hurt'.
God I want to slap the bitch, right in her nasty, disgusting gob! But I need to keep my wits about me and stay calm, because unbeknown to her, I had the recorder going on my phone, which is in my pocket. I have recorded the cow admitting to lying.
Once James hears it, I know he will sort her out once and for all. I need to get out of here now though, as quickly as possible.

'Right, well, I guess I should be going then. See you around ... or not. Whatever. I got what I came for, which was the truth. So, I'll leave you to it then'. I rushed out of there, as fast as my feet would carry me. Thankfully the elevator doors were just opening when I reached them, so I jumped in and repeatedly hit the ground floor button quickly. Ricky was waiting for me outside to take me back home and to make sure I had got the recording.
Outside, he was waiting by the car. I rushed over to him and took my phone out of my pocket.

'Did you get the recording? Please tell me you got it Belle'.
I smiled up at him and nodded.

'Are you fucking serious?'

'As a heart attack. Let's get out of here and back to my place so we can listen to it ... god Ricky, James is going to flip when he hears it, you are too. You are not going to believe the crap she was trying to pull'.
We jumped in his car and as he started the engine and we set off, he shook his head and quickly glanced my way.

'What Ricky?'

'Are you still going to go through with the marriage plan, I mean, after all this shit with Davina?'

'Yeah, why wouldn't I?'
The look he gave me then, told me that he wasn't so sure about my decision. But I was ok about it, especially now after the stunt that bitch tried to pull in front of the board. She probably had no idea about the ultimatum they had given to James, but still, she had thrown a major spanner in the works. One that could have cost him his company. I was damned if I was going to let that happen.

'Look Belle. I love you to the moon and back, you know that, and the last thing I want is for you to get hurt. But this plan of my brothers is only going to cost you heartache. I know you think you are only doing it, because you want to help him. But we both know the real truth here. You love him. You have been in love with him since we were kids'.

THE SEXY FAKER

'Look Ricky, I know what you think to be true, but it just isn't. That was years ago, I don't feel that way anymore. Besides, I have had a few relationships since then. What I am doing for James is because I love him as a friend. My *best friend* and it is what *best friends* do for each other, help them out in time of need'.

Ricky looks at me intently before speaking. 'Who are you trying to convince Belle, me or yourself?'

Crap! He's right, who the hell am I trying to convince?

'Let us just get back to my place, so you can listen to the recording'.

Ricky's hands rub over his face, as he paces back and forth in my living room. After listening to the recording of Davina's confession, the contempt in his face is obvious.

We have been at my apartment for the last thirty minutes and sipping on beers.

'I can't believe that bitch would do something like this to James. What the fuck did he do to hurt her so badly, that she would attempt to ruin him like that?'

'You mean, other than fuck her, and then dump her ass for cheating on him? And leaving the country to get away from her? I have no idea'. I'm sorry, I couldn't help my voice drip with sarcasm. So, sue me!

'We need to call James over now and have him hear this'. He starts to get his phone out of his pocket.

I hold my hand up to stop him.

'Wait. I am having dinner with him tonight. I was going to play it for him then'.

'What, in the middle of dinner, with people all around you? I don't think that is the best idea Belle. He is going to flip. It is better he hears this now. I will call him and tell him to come over'. He scrolls through his contacts just as my phone goes off too.

When I look at who is calling, I'm shocked.

'I have to take this Ricky, I'll go in my room'. I click answer. 'Mr Bilton, what an unexpected surprise'.

'Yes, I guess it is. How are you Annabelle?'

'I'm good, thanks. What can I do for you sir?'

'Well, it is more that, what I can do for you. Look, Annabelle, I owe you an apology'.

'You do? Why is that sir?'

'Because I should have gone with my gut instinct and believed what you told me. I should never have listened to the twaddle Kent Draxton said about you. For that I am truly sorry. The reason I am calling is to ask if you would be willing to come back to us, come back to the firm. That is, if you haven't already found another placement'.

Wow! First of all, Bilton never apologised to anyone. I was honoured. Secondly, did I really want to go back there where that pond scum Draxton was? The answer to that one was a definite NO!

Before I had a chance to reply though, Mr Bilton spoke again.

In fact, I think he must be a mind reader, because he answers the question I was just asking myself.

'Don't worry about Draxton. He no longer works here. After everything, we let him go without recommendation. You won't have to deal with him ever again. So, what do you say Annabelle? Will you come back to the firm, please?'

When I go back in to the living room, Ricky is staring down at his phone looking ...confused?

'Hey. Is James on his way?'

'Not exactly'. He looks away from me with what looks like embarrassment and is that remorse I saw in his eyes.
What the hell is going on now?

'What do you mean by not exactly Ricky? Is he coming or not?'
He can't even look me in the eye! Why is he turning away from me?
'For fucks sake Ricky. Just tell me!' I bite out.

'I'm not sure I want to'.

'What the hell are you talking about? Wait ... has something happened to him? Tell me now so help me ... I swear to god ...'.

'HE IS WITH HER, OK. THAT BITCH DAVINA, THAT IS WHERE HE IS. SHE ANSWERED HIS PHONE WHEN I RANG. TOOK GREAT PLEASURE IN TELLING ME THAT THEY HAD JUST FUCKED AND WAS IN THE SHOWER. THAT HE HAD FORGIVEN HER AND TOOK HER BACK ... THERE, HAPPY NOW?'

No. That didn't sound right at all. No way was he with her. No way would he ever take her back. Something didn't add up.

'But, we just left there. You must be mistaken. He would never take her back'.

'Then how come she answered his phone? How the fuck do you explain that one Annabelle? I knew he would do this, hurt you. I told him not to bother coming back, but no, he wouldn't listen to me'. Ricky tugs at his hair, while I just stare at him dumbfounded.

'What the hell Ricky! You told him not to come back home, like ever? How could you? He's your brother and he's my …'. I trailed off because, well, I didn't need to say out loud just what James meant to me. Ricky already knows anyway, so what would be the point. He thinks I am hurt again, but I know there must be more to it. That James is not really taking Davina back. Something more must be going on as to why she answered his phone.
Maybe I am being naïve, who knows. But I have to believe he wouldn't hurt me like that. Not again.

'Look, Annabelle. I just didn't want him coming in and out of your life and upsetting you every time he had to leave again. I was just trying to protect you'.

'You don't need to protect me. I'm a big girl now and I can look after myself. If my feelings get hurt, then so be it. I will do what I have always done, suck it up and move on. Now, why don't we give it another fifteen minutes, then try ringing him again. Find out what the hell is going on'.

'Yeah, ok. Hey, by the way, what was that call about anyway?'

'Oh, right. That was Mr Bilton. He wants me to come back to the firm. He has apologised and got rid of Mr pervert. So, I said yes'. I couldn't help the beaming grin on my face.
Ricky lunged at me. Picking me up and spinning me around, both of us laughing.
'Wow that's fantastic news Annabelle. When do you start back?'

'Next week. I told him I had a few loose ends to tie up first. But I am so happy to be going back their Ricky. At least now, I can work my way up to partner without that scumbag throwing spanners in the works at every opportunity like before. I know, let's crack open that special bottle of champers I have been saving. This classes as a special occasion, right?'

'Hell, yeah it does'.

Everything was starting to work out great for once. I just needed to know that James and I were on the same page. Maybe I should call him instead of Ricky. But what if she answers again, she said James knows everything, but I very much doubt that. I could threaten to tell him if she didn't put him on the phone. I could …
My phone lights up. The caller name flashing. James.

'Hey James'.

'Belle, I need to speak to you. Is it ok if I come to yours now?'

'Sure. Actually, Ricky tried ringing you earlier. I guess Davina got to the phone before you had a chance huh?'

'Fuck! Belle I am so sorry, but it is not what you think. I wasn't with her in that way ... look I will explain everything when I get there. See you soon'.

Ricky looked at me. His brow furrowed.
'Was that my brother?'

'Yeah. He's on his way here. Said Davina picking up the phone wasn't what I thought. Apparently, he will explain everything when he gets here'.
I plop down on the sofa. Ricky sits next to me and grabs my hand, lifting it to his lips and kissing my knuckles. I let out a sigh. I need to relax, because I know there is nothing going on between James and Davina. That it is just her way of manipulating the situation. I am sure James will have a good explanation as to why he was at her hotel room, and then we can move on.

THE SEXY FAKER

JAMES

I had to make it clear, once and for all to Davina, that I was never getting back with her. She could stay in the hotel for as long as needed until I got that damn paternity test done. I was going to make sure that if the child was mine, I would provide it. Though it may sound harsh, I hoped to fuck the baby wasn't mine, because it was a complication I didn't need right now.

I knock on the door of Davina's hotel room. I had texted her ten minutes ago to tell her I was coming to see her. She never replied, so I am hoping she is in.

I am still holding the phone in my hands, when the door swings open. She is wearing a hotel bath robe, the bump visible underneath.

'Hi James. I'm glad you text. Sorry I didn't reply right away but I was taking a shower. Come in, can I get you something to drink?'

I shake my head. I needed a clear head for this and alcohol was the last I wanted. What I did want, was to get out of here as quickly as possible and get ready for my date with Belle.

'Do you mind if I do, it's been a long day'. I am shocked to see her filling a glass up with red wine.

'WHAT THE FUCK DO YOU THINK YOU ARE DOING DAVINA! I WILL NOT HAVE YOU DRINKING IF YOU ARE CARRYING MY BABY'. I couldn't help shouting at her. How dare she put the baby at risk like that. Even if it isn't mine, it is still wrong to drink when you are pregnant.

'Oops. I wasn't thinking, sorry. I promise I haven't touched a drop. Maybe you should drink this one, it is a shame to waste it now that it's been poured'. She saunters over to me and holds out the glass to me. Only when I reach for it, she trips on the rug and the wine splashes all over me.

'God damn it Davina!'

'James, I am so sorry'. She gasps. 'Why don't you go in to the bathroom and clean up'.
I place my phone in my blazer pocket and remove it, draping it over a chair before heading in to the bathroom. I lock the door behind me, because the last thing need is for her to get any ideas and come in here when I am in nothing but my boxers.
I rinse out the stained patch on the front of my shirt, then grab a towel off the rail, damp it and proceed to wipe the wet patch on the bottom of my trousers. What a mess! I am pretty sure she did it on purpose to get me undressed. Too bad for her I have my wits about me and locked the fucking bathroom door.
When I finish up and exit the bathroom after getting dressed

again. Davina is sitting on the edge of the bed, sipping from a bottle of water.

'Look, Davina. I need to make sure you understand that there is nothing between us anymore. That we won't ever be getting back together. Once the DNA has been done to determine if the baby is mine, then we can discuss what happens next, but only in regard to the child and not us. Do you understand what I am saying?'

'It's her isn't it? That tart who was at the party. What does she have that I haven't James? I thought we had something good together, you know we are made for each other. Why can't you just admit it, so we can fly back to L.A and be together. We can get married and bring up our baby instead of living in different countries and our child having to fly back and forth ... come on James, you know it makes sense'.
She stands from the bed and wraps her arms around my neck and plants her lips on mine, before I can blink.
Just as quickly, I grip her wrists and unwind her from me, gently back stepping her towards the bed. The backs of her knees hit the bed, forcing her to sit.

'Don't ever talk about Belle that way again. In fact, don't even think about her, and don't ever touch me again either. We are done here. Do you understand me?'
I spin on my heel. I need to leave here right now, because as much as I have never had even an inkling to hit a woman, she is certainly pushing my buttons. Just thinking it makes me feel sick, because I would be first in line to kick the shit out of

any man that laid a finger on a woman. But as I reach for the door knob, her words stop me.

'I will tell her you were here. That we fucked, and you want me back. I will ruin your stupid little ... whatever it is you are doing with her, and from what I could gather from your friends at the party, they weren't too pleased about you having a fiancée with child and bringing another woman to the party. So, I suggest you think long and hard about us and make the right decision'.

Like I said, I have never hit a woman, but she is begging for it. I clench my jaw as tight as my fists and leave the room. Outside the hotel I take my phone out and call Belle. I need to speak to her now, before Davina as a chance to and explain everything.

I have come a long way for this plan to dissolve before my very eyes, thanks to Davina. On Monday, I will explain the Davina situation and hope they understand. Hope that they believe me in that it is Belle I plan on marrying.

When I eventually get off the phone with Belle, I am fuming. Davina! That conniving devious bitch answered my phone while I was in the bathroom cleaning up!

It sounds like Richard is there too, so it saves me telling my side of things twice instead of just once, thank fuck.

He's sat on the sofa drinking a bottle of beer when Belle let's me in. I kiss her on the cheek. She didn't flinch or pull away, which is a good sign.

Richard on the other hand is scowling at me. His lips pursed, like he wants to say something.

Out of the corner of my eye I see shaking her head at him when his eyes drift toward her.

'Right, so about that phone call that Davina answered. I need to explain what happened and it is not what you think … yes, I was there at her hotel room but only to have a conversation with her. I needed her to understand that I have no intentions of taking her back and if the baby is mine, then of course I would provide for it. I also …'. I pause then, because they give each a look with raised eyebrows. 'What?' I look at each one of them.

'Well …'. Belle starts to say slowly. Richard holds his hand up and picks Belle's phone up off the coffee table. He scrolls and fiddles with it for a few seconds. Then I hear the distinct voice of Belle.

'What is that?' I am confused. Why am I listening to a recording of Belle … wait is that Davina?

'Shut up James, for fucks sake and listen'. I blanch at the venom in his voice. But as I listen, I begin to understand why, and my blood is boiling to a temperature high enough to erupt like a volcano.
That bitch isn't even pregnant! She has been lying to me all this time. Making me believe that I could possibly be a father, even if I had hoped the baby wasn't mine. I would have made good damn sure I was the best father in the world if it was mine.
Now that choice had been taken away from me. I know I should have felt relieved at the fact I was in the clear. But

honestly, all I felt was betrayal and a little hurt that someone could play me like that.

All I did was end a relationship that wasn't working. I didn't love her, and it was made pretty clear she didn't love me, when I caught her fucking someone else. So, I don't understand her hatred of me to do something like this, and for what? To hurt me! I just don't get it. I am not a bad person. I used to think so, years ago. It took me being in therapy to convince me that I wasn't a bad man like my father. That just because that scum of the earths blood ran through my veins didn't mean I was like him.

But this. Davina was dead to me now. There was nothing she could do to me. But I sure as hell could do a lot to her and I will ruin her deceitful ass!

After the recording ended, I slumped down on the sofa next to Richard. Belle leaned over and handed me a beer. Closing my eyes, it felt like a heavy weight had been lifted from my shoulders.

'James, what the fuck happened at the hotel, why did she answer your phone?' My brother bit out.

'She accidently on purpose spilled red wine on me ...' I waved my hand at the red stain down my shirt. 'My phone was in my blazer pocket which I slung over a chair while I went in to the bathroom to clean up. That is when I assume you rang and she answered the phone ... Belle, I am so sorry, you have to believe me when I say nothing happened between me and Davina. I wouldn't do that to you sweetheart, I would never cheat on you. Please trust that I am telling you the truth. I

love you and you are the only one I want to be with'.
Richard's eyes are wide. I take Belle's hands in mine and kiss her palms.

'You told her you love her?' Richard shakes his head, but then a wide smile creeps on his face.
Belle leans in to me and I pull her on to my lap, cradling her face and kissing her softly.

'Right guys and gals, that is my que to leave. James, let me know what you're going to do about Davina. Whatever it is, I am in'. He does a two fingered salutes and leaves.

'James'. She whispers breathlessly in my ear.

'Belle'. I croak out. Because my emotions are getting the better of me. I don't just love her, I adore her. I am obsessed with her.
I have never been as happy as I am now, and it is all because of her. My Belle.
'Belle, do you believe what I said? Do you trust me?'

'Yes James, I do. I love you too, so very much. I never thought you would ever feel the same way, that is why I have been holding back from telling you. I didn't want to make a fool of myself. You see, I have loved you since we were kids and when you left ….'. She takes a deep breath before continuing. 'When you left, my heart broke in to a million pieces. It took me years to get over you, or so I thought. Now, well now, I don't think I ever did'.

'I am so, so sorry I left like I did. I wish I could go back and at least say goodbye to you'.

'Why did you leave like that James. I know it must have been something bad for you to up and leave. I just didn't understand at the time. Ricky told me he didn't know, but I am guessing he did, does know'. I nod slowly. My brother knows everything about that night and why I had to leave. It took him a long time to forgive our mother for her lies. I never did, not until she died.

I guess now is the time to tell Belle everything. I move her off my lap to sit next to me.

'I supposes now is as good as any to tell everything that happened that night and why I had to leave'. I take a few deep breaths and begin to tell her my story.

'The night of your birthday party. The night we almost kissed. Well, after I left your house, I really didn't feel like going out with the guys, so I ended up going home. When I got there, mum was drunk and waving what looked like a letter in her hands. She was mumbling something about a dead beat and a fucking loser and why was he writing her letters now.

She didn't see me at first, but when she spun around and saw me stood at the door watching her, she pointed her finger at me. Said I was juts like him and wished she had an abortion when she found out she was pregnant with me, then that bastard wouldn't have any ties.

I had no clue what the hell she was talking about. She threw the letter at me and stumbled away to her bedroom. So, I picked it up and read the letter. It was from a guy called Gerry Fortune. My father'.

'What? No, that can't be right. Your dad's name was Bill. I remember you and Ricky talking about him'.

'Bill was Richards dad, not mine. Turns out my father or sperm donor I should say, was a criminal. A murdering scumbag who was in prison since before I was even born. My mum was six months pregnant with me when he killed someone and ended up with a life term. Of course, mum never told me any of this, she was too drunk to tell me anything. So, I took it upon myself to find out all about him. I travelled to America, because that is where he was imprisoned, in one of the high security facilities there in California ... I used all my savings to find a cheap motel nearby the prison, then after a few days of trying to build up the courage, I just thought fuck it. I came all this way to find out the truth. So, I went the next day. Luckily, he knew who I was and excepted my visit'. I look up at her then, to see how she was reacting, but she was just looking down at out joined hands.

Was she even listening to me?
'Belle?'

'I'm listening James. I guess I'm just taking it all in. Please, go on'.

I take another deep breath. But I can't carry on without a drink. I need something stronger than beer though.

'Do you have anything stronger than beer? I could use a proper drink'.

'Sure, there's some Jack Daniels in the drink cabinet'.
After pouring myself a drink, gulp it down then pour another.
I lift the glass to Belle, seeing if she wants one too, but she
shakes her head no., so I go back and sit down next to her.
Placing the glass on the coffee table, I begin again with my
story.

'He knew who I was the minute he walked in. He came
straight up to the table where I was sitting and held his hand
out to shake it. But I couldn't do it, I just stared up at him,
because it was like looking at myself in twenty years' time.
His hair was longer than mine, but his facial features and hair
and eye colour were the same as mine. I couldn't believe it,
this murdering bastard was my blood. It was odd too,
because when he spoke, he was ... nice? Yeah, I know it
sounds weird, don't get me wrong I knew he had killed
someone and that doesn't make you a nice person.
All the time I was sat there though, all I could think about was
that I was a nice person too, and would I eventually kill
another human being like he did. Would I be that preverbal
"chip off the old block" and turn out like him.
That is why I stayed away for so long. When I left after that
one and only visit with my father, I knew I had to do
something to make me a better person. I didn't want to wake
up one day in a prison cell. I needed to prove to myself and
to you, that I was a good person. A good enough man to be
with you, because you deserved to be with someone who
wasn't a bastard'. I cup her face and bring my lips to meet

hers, kissing her tenderly. Her cheeks are damp from the tears that I have just noticed, so I kiss the salty wetness away.

'James. You are a good person, a good man. You have always been good enough for me, don't ever think any differently. Not now. You are nothing like your father. Like you said, he was just a sperm donor. But without him, I wouldn't have you. I love you so much and I believe in you and that this plan of yours will work'.

I pull her on to my lap. My lips clash harsh on to hers. I needed to hear her say those words to me, more than anything.

I took a loose strand of hair behind her ear and slowly move my hands down her back, cupping her perfect round ass. She starts to grind against my erection, making me even harder, I can't stand it any longer, I need more. I lift her up and carry her to the bedroom, closing the door with my foot. I lay her down on the bed and lay on top of her. Kissing her neck, I make my way down, lifting the hem of her top up and over her head.

She shimmies her pants down, leaving her in just her bra and panties. I take off my blazer and shirt and lean over her, taking her lips again, biting and sucking on her bottom one, before trailing kisses down her neck and across her clavicle.

'James. More, I need more, please'. She begs in a whisper. So, I strip her of her bra and panties and throw them on the floor behind me. Licking my lips at the sight of her wet pussy. I make short work of removing the rest of my clothes.
I get on the bed and position myself between Belle's legs.

Cupping her breasts, I take a nipple in to my mouth, while I flick and pinch the other with my finger and thumb.
I trail kisses from her breast to her stomach, as my hand travels down and I slip two fingers inside her.
Her body jerks with each thrust of my fingers, my pace quickening the harder she clamps down on them. Her body tremble as she calls out my name.
I pull back my fingers when she calms and take hold of my cock, sheathing myself with a condom, then easing inside her slow giving her time to adjust to me.
As I slide in and out of her, I pick up the pace and grip her hips. Lifting up her leg over my shoulder. The new angle allowing me to push deeper inside of her.
Her moans turn in to screams and an intense orgasm rocks through her.
I pump faster, chasing my own release. Sweat trickling down my forehead and back with each thrust.
Needing her to come again, I reach between us and press my thumb to her clit, circling. I feel her walls clench my cock, shouting out my name. I lean down and kiss her as my body trembles with my own explosive orgasm.
I pull out and fall to the side, wrapping my arms around her and pulling her to me. I kiss her temple and sigh.
This is what I want. I want forever and from this day forward she will be by my side every day.

'I love you Belle'.

'I love you too James'.

JAMES

Even though Mondays are supposed to be the worse day of the week. I couldn't help having a spring in my step as I made my way to work.
I knew the board members were waiting for me, but I didn't give a flying fuck. I was happy because me and Belle were finally together. We had declared our love for each other and nothing and no-one could change that. The other fantastic news was that she had got her job back. They had finally come to their senses and got rid of that scheming scumbag pervert. So, at least I knew she would be fine working their now, without me having to commit bodily harm to that fucker every day for touching her.
Whatever the board had to say, well, they could ram it up their arses. Because I knew, that once I told them everything about Davina and her lies, and about my feelings for Belle, that all would be ok.
So, I whistled as I walked through the office and straight to the board room, where they were all sat waiting for me.

'What are you so happy about?' Kenny, my right-hand man asked.

'Love Kenny, that is what I am happy about'. I continued on my way.

Everyone was sat at the big oval table in the conference room waiting for me.

I take a seat at the end and wait to be broached.

'Thank you for coming in so early James. Now, let us get down to business. I do believe that you are already engaged and soon to be a father. So, I suggest ...'.

I cut him off. 'That isn't exactly true Trevor'. I remove invisible lint from my trousers.

'What are you talking about James?' This came from Jason.

'I mean there is no baby. Davina not only lied to you, but to me too. She had me believe she was pregnant, but there was a chance it might not have been mine any way. I was going to get a DNA done after the child was born. Turns out there is no baby to start with. Davina is not pregnant ... oh, and we were never engaged either. She was a fling I had back in L.A and I ended it when I caught her cheating on me'.

They whispered loudly among themselves before addressing me again.

'We still can't allow your behaviour to continue. We specifically said we needed to see a change otherwise we would vote you out of the company. We think that ...'

'Let me just stop you right there Trevor. Look, I know in the past I haven't been the best CEO or role model for my company. But all that has changed. I wasn't lying to you when I told about Belle. I did ask her to marry me and we are engaged. She is the love of my life. I have loved her since we were kids. Coming back here, home. I realised when we reconnected, that I never stopped loving her all these years. So, you can do what you like. Kick me out, I don't care. All I care about is Belle and I can't wait to make her my wife'. I shoved my chair back and stood up to leave.

'Wait!' Eric called out. He hardly ever spoke. He was the quiet one of the board. So, when he told me to wait, I did. My heart was pounding so hard I could hear it.

'I'm waiting' I said, arching my brow. I didn't know what to expect. They could still easily kick me out if they wanted to. I really hoped they didn't though. I stood firm, my back straight, waiting on my fate.

'I think we made a mistake. You've done what we asked you do. Now, let us move forward. So, James, when is the big day? Our wives are extremely excited about the wedding'.

After seeing the board out. I sat back in my chair in my office and contemplated what had happened in my life up to this point.
Finding out at the age of eighteen that the man who had brought me up for the first few years of my life, wasn't my birth father. My real father was a man who was a criminal. A murderer.
The lies my mother told me over and over, making me believe that Richards dad had also been mine.
Working damn hard to get to where I am today. Starting a

business from scratch is hard to do.
But the hardest thing I ever had to do in my life, was leave Belle behind. I had to make sure I wasn't anything like my real father, that his bad blood didn't run through my veins. Once I accomplished that, I knew it was time to come back and make Belle mine. We had now come full circle.
Belle's ring tone sounded loud as it drew me from my daydream.

'Hey sweetheart, this is a surprise. I only left you a couple of hours ago. What, are you missing me already? I can ...'. But before I can say anything else, a gruff male voice bellows at me to shut the fuck up.
What the hell!
'Who the hell are you, and why are you answering my fiancées phone?'

'Sir, I am sorry for shouting and swearing at you, but you wouldn't let me get a word in. My name is DCI Cooper and I found you on her phone as in case of emergency contact. I'm afraid your fiancée has been involved in a series car accident ...'.

'FUCK! IS SHE OK? WHAT HOSPITAL HAVE THEY TAKEN HER TO? TELL ME'. I felt sick. My hands trembled as I tried to stay calm. I was already out the door with my car keys in my hand, running towards my car. Kenny called after me, but I couldn't stop. I had to get to Belle. Fuck! If anything happened to her I would die a thousand deaths to be with her.

THE SEXY FAKER

'Sir, she is at St Marys. The air ambulance has just left with her. The fire service had to cut her out of the car'.

'Detective, please for the love of god, tell me what happened. I am going crazy here'.

The Detective let out a deep sigh. He must have heard the panic in my voice though because he began to tell me what happened.
'Sir, it looks like someone ran her off the road. There are skids marks to suggest she tried to break. Secondary tire tracks confirm that her car was pushed over the barrier and in to the water. Luckily a driver passing in the opposite direction and saw her car go over. They call 999 then jumped in to save her, but she was trapped. He kept her head above the water line in an air pocket inside the car until the emergency services turned up fifteen minutes later'.

'I want the guys name. To thank him'. I drove as fast as I could, if I got pulled over then they could fuck off and arrest me after I had seen Belle and made sure she was ok.

'He was taken to the hospital also. I am sure you can catch him there. I'll be a long too shortly to take statements from your fiancée and the gentlemen who helped save her'.
I ended the call with a thank you and double parked outside the hospital. I didn't care if I got a ticket or towed. Belle is all that mattered. Once I knew she was ok, then I would find the fucker who ran her off the road and I will kill them with my bare hands.
Everyone looked at me as I charged through the hospital, but

THE SEXY FAKER

I didn't give a shit what people thought about me. I needed to get to Belle. Fuck! I needed to let Richard know what has happened too.

I find my way to the right area, just as they are wheeling her in through the double doors. Her eyes are closed. She has a neck and back support. I can blood on her face and her clothes look like they have been ripped to shreds.

They rush past me. I call her out name, even though I know she probably can't hear me, but I need her to know that I am here.

A guy in scrubs is talking to me. I don't have a clue what he is saying. I have blanked out any sounds around me, all I can hear is my own heart beating rapidly. A sharp pain in my chest as I clutch the front of my shirt. I can't breathe. I stagger back in to the wall behind me and slide down to the floor. Is this what a heart attack feels like?

A bright light is shone in to my eyes. A mask is placed over my mouth and nose. I take in long deep breaths until I feel myself turning back to normal. I look around and see the guy in scrubs knelt in front of me and a nurse stood next to him.

'That's it buddy. Long deep breaths. You're getting there. How do you feel now?' The guy in scrubs concerned face peers at me, and I remove the mask from my face.

'What happened?' I ask, as I look around to see where they took Belle.

'You had a panic attack and fainted. Here, sip this'. He hands me a glass a water and helps me up off the floor.

'My fiancée, she was brought in. Car accident. Do you know where they have taken her?'

The nurse looked at the guy in scrubs and shook her head. What was that? I balled my fists. Belle wasn't dead, if that is what she is insinuating.

'Are you sure she was brought here sir?' Guy in scrubs asks.

'I am sure, I just saw her brought in before I collapsed. Please, can you find out where they took her. I need to see her'.

'No-one has been brought through here for the last hour'.

'What? I have been out for an hour? Fuck! I need to go find her'. I try to push past him, but he grabs my arm.

'Sir, why don't you tell me her name and I'll see what I can find out. Come on, take a seat in here and I'll grab you some coffee too'.

I tell him her name and he leaves me in what looks to be a family room. The place where relatives wait to be told the bad news about their loved ones.

I sit down on one of the sofa's and put my head in my hands. I can't fucking believe this. Belle is not dead. I would feel it if she were, I know I would.

I get up and start to pace. My anxiety levels are peaking and I still haven't contacted my brother yet to tell him what's happened to Belle.

Scrubs guy walks in with a steaming mug of black coffee. Perfect.

'Hey. So, I found out where your fiancée is. She was taken straight in to surgery when she arrived, due to some internal bleeding. They managed to stop it though, so that is great news. Unfortunately, they think there may have been some nerve damage to her lower back. At this moment in time, I am afraid she is paralyzed and there is no way of knowing if it is temporary or permanent. The surgeon and specialists are positive that she will make a full recovery regarding all other injuries. She has a concussion, a broken arm and ankle'. His low soft tone was supposed to be comforting. It would have been to anyone else too. But all I heard was she was paralyzed. I needed to see her, to talk to her. Let her know I was here and wasn't going anywhere. I would be by her side no matter what. That is what marriage is all about. For better for worse. In sickness and in health.

'Is she conscious?'

'Not yet, she is still in recovery, but I can take you there, so you can sit with her. I am sure your face is the first thing she will want to see. Is there any other family I can contact for you?'

'Yeah, my brother Richard. I was going to do it, but …'. My words drift off because I still feel dazed about everything.

'Give me his contact details and I will make sure he get's the information'.
I give him Richards phone number and follow him out of the room and through the vast corridors to where Belle's room is.

THE SEXY FAKER

I gasp when I walked in and see the state of her. Wires are hooked up to her. An oxygen mask covers her face. Her arm is in a cast and there is a bandage wrapped around her head. Her eyes are black and blue. The beeping of the machines is annoying but a comfort, because it means that her heart is still beating. She is fighting to stay around.
I sit in the chair next to the bed and take her hand in mine. Her skin feels warm and clammy. Another good sign.
I stroke the back of her hand with thumb. Gently caressing, hoping she can feel my touch.

'Wake up Belle. Please wake up. I love you so damn much and I am not going anywhere. I'm here, just ... wake up for me, so we can get married. You know that takes planning and I am no good at shit like planning a wedding, so you have to wake up and get better, because we both know you will do a better job at it than me'.

I am not exactly sure how long I sat there, my head laid on the bed and holding her hand. It could have been minutes or hours for all I care, I wasn't going anywhere until she woke up.

I heard the door to her room open, but I was too tired to lift my head. It was probably just the nurse coming to check on Belle again.

It wasn't until I heard the audible gasp of "Jesus fucking Christ" That I lifted my head and saw my brothers bottom lip trembling.

'Hey, how is she doing?'

THE SEXY FAKER

'I ...'. I clear my throat because I am not sure how to answer that, so I take a deep breath and tell him that bad part first. 'She's paralyzed, and they don't know yet if it will be permanent or not. She also has a concussion, that's why she is unconscious at the moment. She was knocked out and hasn't come to yet. They have done an MRI and there is no bleeding or swelling on the brain. So, they aren't too concerned about that. It is just a waiting game'.

'Fuck! What do you need me to do bro?'

'Just be here. If the paralysis is permanent, she is going to need us both. I will fly in the best damn specialist team in this field to help her. Get whatever she will need so she can keep her independence'.

'You still want to marry her?'

I stand up abruptly and face off with him. What the fuck! 'What kind of a fucking question is that? How dare you think that I would abandon her just because she has lost the use of her legs! Yes, it is going to be difficult at first, but I love her, and she will be my wife, no matter what. Now, get the fuck out of here if you are going to come out with dumb shit like that!'

'Look, I'm sorry ok. I didn't mean anything by it. I just thought ... fuck ... I didn't think. James, me and you, we are it for her and I won't let either of you down, I promise. Why don't I go get us some coffee and we can sit next to her and wait for her to wake up together. Back together again, just like when we were kids'. He squeezes my shoulder and leave, closing the door quietly behind him.

I finally let out the breath I hadn't realised I was holding and go sit back down. Taking Belle's hand in mine once again. When Richard comes back with coffees and hands me one, he takes a seat at the other side of the bed.

'So, what now James?'

'After Belle has woke up and I know she's going to be ok. We are going to find the bastard that did this to her and kill the fucker'.

'What? I thought she had an accident, a car accident'. He shakes his head.

'According to the detective at the scene and an eye witness. She was run off the road, and when I find whose responsible, I will kill them with my bare hands'. I bite out through gritted teeth. I think I may have to have to see a dentist at this rate, with all the teeth grinding I have been doing lately.

'Shit! Seriously? Who the hell would want to hurt her? She doesn't have any enemies. Maybe it was a case of mistaken identity or something'. Richards stands and starts pacing back and forth.

'Doesn't matter. The fucker will pay for it when I get my hands on them'.

'Right. In the meantime, what can I do?'

'Do you still have that friend that works at the police station?' He nods. 'Can you find out what the witness saw? I was too out of it and worried about Belle earlier to seek him out. He was brought here too after he saved her. I need to know everything. Can you do that for me?'

'Sure. Absolutely. I'll go now and see what I can find out about the acci ... I mean incident and get back to you asap'.

After he left, my attention was all on Belle again. I have never been a religious man, but I prayed for her to wake. Because at this point I would try anything.
I must have fallen asleep at some point, because I was awakened by a tickling on my cheek. I swatted at whatever it was, but it wouldn't go away. As I slowly came around, I remembered where I was and began to open my eyes. When I looked up, Belle was staring back at me with a wide grin on her face.
I abruptly sat up and rubbed my eyes, to make sure I was actually awake and not dreaming.

'You're awake'.

'Yeah, I woke up a few minutes ago. I didn't mean to wake you up. You look tired'.

'Do you remember what happened to you, why you are in the hospital?' I gulped down the hard lump in my throat and stroked a finger down her cheek. Cupping her chin softly.

'Yes James, I remember. I also know who it was that run me off the road. It was ...'
But before she had chance to finish the sentence, Richard came barging through the door, talking excitedly.

'James, I found out who it was that tried to kill Annabelle … Shit! Hey Annabelle, great to see you awake. You had everyone worried there. How are you feeling sweetheart?'

'Ok I guess. I know who did this and I suppose you do too Ricky? Why don't we say it together and see if we have the same person?'

'Belle, just say who it was, please'. I caressed her cheek and looked over at Richard. It was more important to me that she knew who did this. Richards guy may have reliable, but I didn't know him. It wasn't a guarantee that they found the right scumbag.
Belle smiled down at me, then looked over at Richard still stood by the door.

'On three … one … two … three …. Kent Draxton …'

'Kent Draxton …'
They both said the same name together. That dirty pervert from her work had done this, and I was going to make him pay. I stood up, knocking the chair over.

'I am going to kill him' My jaw tensed as I charged across the room towards the door.

'James, wait. You can't just go after him. We have to call the police and let them deal with him. Please James, come and sit back down, right now I need you … and I … something is weird, and I think I need to see the doctor. Ricky can you go get the doctor for me please'.
I reach for her and cup her face. I can see the distress she is hiding behind her eyes. I know she must realise that she can't

move her legs. The fear on her face and tears in her eyes are ripping my heart to shreds.

'Sweetheart, I know this will be hard, but remember I am here to support you and Richard is too. We will help you get through this'. I kiss her gently on the lips as a single fat tear runs down her cheek. I wipe it away with my thumb and kiss her again, to show her how much I love her.
She sobbed in to my neck as I held her tightly.
The door swung open and in walked Richard, followed by the doctor, and then a nurse.

'It is good to finally see you awake Annabelle. The nurse here is just going to take all your vitals, then we can discuss what is going to happen next. I'll be back a couple of minutes'.

'James, don't leave until the doctor has been back'.

'I am going no-where sweetheart. I promise you that'. I take her hand in mine and stroke it gently, while her sobs subside. The doctor comes back and looks at an ipad in his hands, then looks up and smiles. Ok ... so him smiling is a good sign, right? Or am I just trying to be optimistic here?

'Right, so it's good news Annabelle. We were a little concerned about paralysis in your legs, but after looking over the scans and the two MRI we did. I can see that there is no damage to the spine, it appears that you have a trapped nerve and that is easily fixed'.
I let out a loud breath I had been holding. It could be fixed. She would be ok and be able to walk.

THE SEXY FAKER

ANNABELLE

It had been three weeks since the accident. Two weeks since the police had found Kent Draxton and arrested him for dangerous driving and attempted murder with a motor vehicle.

I was recovering well from the trapped nerve and was eager to get back to work. James however, had other ideas. According to him, he wasn't going to risk losing me again and had taken time off work to care for me around the clock. I constantly called him my babysitter which he hated, which only made me laugh. I was so used to taking care of myself, that it felt odd to have someone take over that job, even if I did love him with all my heart.

Ricky came over from time to time and kept me relatively sane, by plying me with beer and blueberry muffins.

Mr Bilton, bless him, was holding my job open and told me to take as long as I needed to get back to 100%. Everyone at the firm had also clubbed together to send me a gift basket of the most expensive and exquisite skin and toiletry products, as well as a get well soon card. Which was really sweet of them.

James was in full wedding mode now too. He was

determined that the wedding would go ahead no matter what.

I was just happy. So, so happy right now that I felt like I was floating on a white fluffy cloud surrounded by cute little lambs bleating cheery tunes all around me.

Yeah, I think the pain meds have finally kicked in, because my brain has gone all floopy.

Loud knocking brings my haze in to focus and I groan, because I have to move and I have just gotten comfy on the sofa.

I drag myself up and walk over to answer the door. It could only be one of the neighbours because James and Ricky were at work.

I look through the peephole to see which one of the nosy neighbours it is. But it is no-one I recognize, maybe the guy is a new resident.

I open the door his back is to me and he turns when he hears the door open and flashes me a Hollywood smile.

Oh, fuck me now! This man was gorgeous. I think I just died and went to heaven. I must have, because no man should be that pretty in real life.

'Hi there, I'm here to see James. Could you tell him he has a visitor by the name of Kristof Venti'.

That voice? Oh my god! It dripped of sex and ... other stuff.

'Ahh ... um ... yeah ... so not here. James, I mean, he's not here. Can I help you with something? I am his fiancée Annabelle. Or, you could come back later, he should be home around five. I mean that's if you want to of course'. I let out a loud sigh, because what the hell was wrong with me? Why was I acting like a star struck hormonal teenage girl? Especially when I am engaged to the love of my life. In my defence, it is ok to look as long as that is all it is. It's not like I want to jump on this guy Kristof. But holy guacamole, he is hot.

'That wont work for me I am afraid. I have to fly back to Italy in a few hours. Here, take this and have him call me'.
He hands me a small card with his name and contact details emblazoned in sliver metallic writing.

'Will he know who you are?'

'No, but he will. Goodbye Ms Annabelle, it was a pleasure to meet you'.
He turned, and I watched him walk away. Even his exit was sexy.
James comes home dead on five o'clock. I was napping on the sofa when I heard the key in the door.

'Hey beautiful, how was your day?'

'Good and weird'.

'Weird, how so?' he shrugs his suit jacket over the back of the sofa and sits down next to me, pulling my legs over his knee.

'Some guy dropped by, left his card and wants you to call him'. I hand him the card.

'Kristof Venti? I don't know who that is. Did he say anything else to you, about what he wanted?'

THE SEXY FAKER

I shake my head. 'Nope. Just said he needed to speak to you. Oh, yeah, he's flying back to Italy in a few hours. Maybe you should give him a call and find out why he's come from Italy to see you'.

'Probably. Are you ok if I go out again? I really need to know what this guy wants'.

'Sure, I'll be fine. I can start making something to eat and keep it warm until get back'.
He leans down and lightly brushes his lips on my forehead.

'I promise I won't be long. I will text you when I am on my way back home'.
When he leaves I head to the kitchen and start pulling out ingredients and prep the vegetables and chicken.
My mind wanders to Kristof Venti. I wonder who he is and what he wants with James. Maybe he's looking for a property here and someone referenced James. Yeah, that had to be it. I guess I will find out soon enough when he comes home.
I must have fallen asleep on the sofa because when I come to, it is dark outside, and the lights are off. That means that James isn't back yet.
I check the clock on my phone. Ten fifteen. Where the hell is he? I check my phone again, but there are no messages or missed calls.
I scroll through my contacts and ring his number, but it goes straight to voicemail. What the hell! I try again three more times and it goes to voicemail again. So, I text and wait, but after half an hour and no reply, I start to worry.
I am scroll down my contacts again and I am about to call

THE SEXY FAKER

Ricky when the door swings open and a very inebriated James stumbles in.

'What the hell James! Where have you been? I thought something had happened to you. Why didn't you call me or at least answer your phone? ... crap'. I struggle to steady him as he makes his way towards the sofa and crashes down on to it.
I stand in front of him, hands on hips and wait for him to open his eyes and look at me.
When he eventually opens his eyes and looks up at me, he smirks and all I want to do is smack it right off his face.

'What happened James? Why are being like this?'

'I have a brother ...' what the hell is he on about? I know he has a brother, he's called Ricky, my best friend. His words are slurred, and I am so annoyed at him right now, that I storm off in to the bathroom and slam the door.
When I exit the bathroom, he's laid on his back in the middle of the bed. Oh, hell no!

'James, get up. Move! For crying out loud, I want to go to bed'. I take hold of his arm and try to pull him to one side of the bed, but he's a dead weight, passed out on the bed.
Fuck it! I will grab some blankets and go sleep in the spare room and deal with him in the morning.
I am about to leave the bedroom, when I hear his phone ringing. Not even thinking about it, I go over to him and rummage in his pockets to fish it out.
It's an unknown number flashing on the screen. I hit answer

and say hello.
A woman's voice asks for James.

Are you fucking kidding me right now? As he been with another woman getting drunk while I have been stuck here cooking his fucking food?

'I'm sorry but James can't come to the phone right now. May I ask who is calling and take a message'. My tone is so sugary sweet I think I just gave myself cavities.

'Oh, my name is Clare. I work at Petro. I found his wallet when I was cleaning the table he was sat at and it had James contact details. I thought I should let him know I have left it with Gus the owner'.
Shit! Talk about feeling guilty for jumping to conclusions. That James would ever cheat on me, was the stupidest thought I have ever had!

'Right, thanks. I will pass on the message'. I end the call and drop the phone on the bedside table.
Damn him for passing out. He can sleep it off for now, but in the morning, we will be having a serious talk about what happened tonight.

THE SEXY FAKER

JAMES

I feel like I have been hit by a refuse truck. I smell like one too. I daren't even open my eyes yet. Fuck knows if I made it home. It certainly feels like I am laying on a comfy bed, I just hope it is my own and not one of the women that was hitting on me last night.
Fucking Kristof! Why the hell did I allow him to talk me in to going out for a drink? He was supposed to be flying out to Italy but cancelled when I got in touch with him. Said "we have some catching up and bonding to do". All I know is that Belle is going to be pissed at me if I didn't come home last night. Although maybe, I should say less pissed. The food she cooked ruined and me a no show. Yeah, I can't blame her. Just when things were back on track, another surprise falls in my lap. And boy is it a dooby!
Once I can open my eyes and establish where I am, I need to make sure I put things right with Belle. Then I need to get a hold of Richard and tell him the news. Whether he will except it is beyond me. I must say, it took me time and a few whiskeys for it to sink in.
How the hell was I going to tell my half-brother that I had another half- brother without him feeling put out?

Richard was more sensitive than me. I guess he got that from our mother and I got my fathers hard heart. I will just have to make it clear that he will always be my number one brother and just because Kristof had now entered our lives, didn't mean anything would change.

Kristof is ... nothing like our father thank god. His mother is Italian and apparently before he got with my mother, he got with Kristof's mother literally within a few months of each other. So, we are both the same age. He is as shrewd and successful as me when it comes to business matters. He seems to be a great guy too and we got along pretty well from what I can remember about last night.

Shit! I really need to make a move. I slowly open one eye and look around, letting out a sigh of relief when I recognise my bedroom.

I need to get up and have a shower. It should help with this damn hangover. I push myself up on my hands and sit up. Squinting my eyes open fully now. Luckily the curtains are still drawn and not letting much if any, light in to the room. I swing my legs off the bed and steady myself as I stand.

I half expected Belle to be scowling down at me. And thankful that she isn't.

I strip off in the bathroom and stand under the now hot shower. Letting the water burn my skin as I contemplate how to make things right with Belle. I reckon all I have to do is tell her the truth about Kristof and she will understand.

I hang my head. Letting the water cascade over my head and back. My hands on the tiles above supporting me. When I am done, I grab a towel, wrapping it around my waist and then

THE SEXY FAKER

brush my teeth.
Back in the bedroom, I slip in to some sports shorts and a white t-shirt then head out to the kitchen to make myself some coffee.
Belle is no-where to be seen. I check the time on the kitchen clock, when I realise I don't have my phone. Switching the coffee machine on, I go back to the bedroom in search of my phone. I find it on the bed. Scrolling through it I notice some missed calls from my brother and Belle as well as texts and a call from an unknown number. I text Richard to let him know I am good and put the phone in my pocket before going back to the kitchen.
Belle is standing by the coffee machine pouring herself a drink when I enter. She must have heard or sensed me their because her shoulders hunch up.

'Morning Belle ... look, sorry for coming home lat...' she puts up her hand stopping me mid-sentence.

'Don't ... just don't. By the way, the club you were at last night doing god knows what, called last night to say they found your wallet. I suggest you go get it'. She moves to walk passed me, but I grab her arm.

'Listen to me, please. I can explain everything. Will you come sit down so we can talk, it's important'.
She shrugs her, then lets them slump as she goes over to the sofa and sits down. I pour myself a coffee then go over and join her.
'That man who came here yesterday, you remember him?' I continue when she nods. 'Well his name is Kristof Venti and

well ... fuck ... there is no easy way to say this, so I am just going to say it. Kristof is my brother'. Her eyes widen in shock.

'Yeah, that was my reaction too. Apparently, our father was with his mother and mine within a few months of each other. He found out about me a few years ago after his mother died. He was clearing her things out of her home and came across a bunch of letters from my father to her. When he read them, he came to one that said he had a brother. So, he has spent years looking for me. Kristof found my mother, but she would only tell him that I was somewhere in America. He finally managed to track me down here. That was who I was with last night. He cancelled his trip back home to stay a few more days to get to know me. He's invited us and Richard too to have dinner at his hotel tonight ... that is, if you want to. I mean, no pressure'. I wait with bated breath for her to speak. But she looks as stunned as I felt when Kristof told me yesterday.

'So ....' She begins slowly. 'That man, the guy that looks like he came off a catwalk, Hollywood star looky likey ... he is your brother?'

I snap my head around. 'Are you fucking kidding me!' But when I look at her she has a wide grin and a twinkle in her eyes. She's playing with me the little minx.

I tackle her and pin her arms above her head. I kiss her hard. She wraps her legs around my waist, pulling me closer to her. I need her naked beneath me now. I start to undress her. she grabs at my shirt and pulls it up and over my head. I remove

THE SEXY FAKER

her top and begin to pull down her leggings and knickers at the same time. I make swift work of my shorts then plunge in to her because I can't wait any longer. She was already wet enough and we both groan when reach to the hilt, hitting her sweet spot.

I feel her pussy clench as I withdraw then surge forward hard. I take one of her nipples in to my mouth as I continue to thrust in and out of her. She digs her nails in to my taught butt cheeks, urging me to go faster. With every thrust she moans louder and louder. My hips begin to grind against hers as she drags her nails up from my butt and up my back. Digging and scratching. I hiss and pick up speed. Lifting her leg up and bending her knee to her chest, my cock drives in deeper. Our bodies crushed together as her walls clamp down on my cock like a vice when she screams out my name. It is my undoing as my release chases hers. My body trembling as I come and the only sounds that can be heard, are that of us panting, trying to catch our breaths.

I look down in to her eyes and pour out my heart to her, and I don't even care if that makes me soft or soppy.

'The man that I am now, is because of you. I wanted to be a better man for you. I want to be the only man in your heart and mind. The only man to touch you and feel you. I want to be enough for you. The only man you will ever want and need. I love you so fucking much Belle. And my life without you in it ... well I couldn't bear to think about. It is me and you Belle ... it has always been me and you'.

THE SEXY FAKER

'I love you too James, so much. And you have always been enough for me. This is it ... me and you'.

THE END

THE SEXY FAKER

OTHER BOOKS BY MK JUBB

PARADISE CITY
SURRENDER MY HEART
TRUE INTENTIONS
YOU CAN'T RUN FROM LOVE

THE DEADLY SERIES
A Deadly Truth
A Deadly Game

THE SEXY FAKER

THE SEXY FAKER

THE SEXY FAKER

THE SEXY FAKER

THE SEXY FAKER

Printed in Great Britain
by Amazon